It was more than a working relationship

Frankie wrapped her arm around Jules's waist and studied the diagram with him. "I hate to say I told you so...."

"All right, it needs more work." Absently he trailed his fingers over her breast and down her hip, starting a wave of warm fire within her. "So, what do we do now?"

Caught in the sensuous spell of his touch, Frankie swallowed and tried to force her mind back to the problem at hand. "Well, if you add another—"

"No, no," he murmured, tossing the diagram aside and pulling her close. His strong hands cupped the roundness of her derriere and he smiled lazily down at her. "I meant what do *we* do now?"

Dear Reader,

We at Harlequin are extremely proud to introduce our new series, **HARLEQUIN TEMPTATION**. Romance publishing today is exciting, expanding and innovative. We have responded to the ever-changing demands of you, the reader, by creating this new, more sensuous series. Between the covers of each **HARLEQUIN TEMPTATION** you will find an irresistible story to stimulate your imagination and warm your heart.

Styles in romance change, and these highly sensuous stories may not be to every reader's taste. But Harlequin continues its commitment to satisfy all your romance-reading needs with books of the highest quality. Our sincerest wish is that **HARLEQUIN TEMPTATION** will bring you many hours of pleasurable reading.

THE EDITORS

U.S.
HARLEQUIN TEMPTATION
2504 WEST SOUTHERN AVE.
TEMPE, ARIZONA
85282

CANADA
HARLEQUIN TEMPTATION
P.O. BOX 2800
POSTAL STATION "A"
WILLOWDALE, ONTARIO
M2N 5T5

Love Circuits

LEIGH ROBERTS

Harlequin Books

TORONTO • NEW YORK • LONDON
AMSTERDAM • PARIS • SYDNEY • HAMBURG
STOCKHOLM • ATHENS • TOKYO • MILAN

For all the engineers in my life—
keep those circuits humming!

Published July 1984

ISBN 0-373-25120-3

Printed in Canada

"RATS!"

Frankie Warburton put her hands on the hips of her well-faded blue jeans and regarded the overfull rear compartment of her Toyota station wagon with irritation. Heavy pieces of electronic equipment crouched sullenly at the open tailgate. When she'd loaded her microcomputer into the car that morning, she had had to make three trips—one for the disk drive, one for the processor unit and one for the terminal. And now she faced leaving parts of the system unprotected in the car while she carted it piece by piece into the imposing office building before her. She chewed thoughtfully on her lower lip, considering her predicament.

She had pulled her car up as close to the entrance of the building as she could without actually backing through the heavy plate-glass front doors. "Damn bulky cumbersome junk anyway," she grumbled to herself, forgetting for the moment how hard she'd worked to build the system and how attached to it she was. "Guess I'll have to go find a hand truck or at least some extra arms."

Frankie shut the tailgate just as a car pulled into the next parking space. She eyed it appreciatively. Athough she had little time for working on them, she loved well-preserved offbeat autos, and this shiny Morris Minor was in mint condition. She barely noticed the man who climbed out of it until he was halfway to the door.

"Hey! Hey, mister! Just a minute!" She ran after him and caught hold of the faded T-shirt he wore. "Do you work here—at Jones Morton, I mean?"

He turned to face her and she instinctively took her hand from his arm, responding to the frosty look in hazel eyes behind horn-rimmed glasses. "Yes," he said, not giving anything away.

She frowned slightly and almost let him walk off. But as her eyes traveled down to the picture of Shakespeare silk-screened on the front of his T-shirt, she realized that he was adequately muscled for her purposes. "Well, then," she began with a friendly smile, "do you mind helping me carry in some things?" She gestured toward her Toyota wagon. "It's not far."

Some of the ice in his eyes melted. "You want me to carry something?" There was a faint note of incredulity in his voice.

Frankie nodded briskly. "You're not lazy, are you?" This time her smile was definitely teasing. After a moment he smiled back, and something strange happened to Frankie Warburton, who had often and vehemently declared, during the past decade of her twenty-nine years, that love was simply chemistry on a human level, and that her chemistry set was missing the necessary pheromones for it.

She blinked. There was nothing in particular about the man in front of her that couldn't be found in any male specimen, she supposed. Brown hair, nicely wavy, long enough to curl around his ears in a sort of endearing way. Hazel eyes, heavily lashed, behind the studious-looking horn-rimmed frames. All the usual features, arranged agreeably enough in his face. A compact, well-knit body, tanned and lithe. He looked to be in his mid-thirties. She shook her head briefly to clear away the strange, unfamiliar sensation of cloudiness. "My car's over here."

When she opened the tailgate his eyes widened. "Just what—" he began, his puzzled gaze traveling from her straight, slight, jean-clad figure to the equipment in her car. "Are you making a delivery or something? That parking place—"

Still slightly shaken by her unexpected awareness of him, Frankie fought to make the encounter more normal, more like the usual give and take of people united in the common cause of working for a living. "Spots like this are usually already taken by the honchos," she said, lifting out the disk drive and handing it to him. "I was lucky to find it unoccupied. Can you take the processor as well?"

He nodded, but staggered a little when she stacked it on top of the disk drive. Both of the pieces were about the size of stereo components, but heavier. She smothered a smile as he rested his chin on top of the processor unit. "Good. I'll get the terminal and then I won't have to leave anything out here. Sometimes untended equipment can grow legs, and I don't want my system walking off."

She trotted ahead of him and managed to get the door open, holding it with her shoulder as he went through. The receptionist sprang from her seat behind an elaborate chrome-and-glass desk.

"Jules—excuse me, miss, but you'll need a badge—Jules!"

The man kept striding toward a corridor that led off at right angles. "It's all right, Nan. We'll come back for the badge."

Frankie sent an apologetic smile over her shoulder at the distraught receptionist. She should have realized there would be security measures. Badges and checkpoints were standard procedure at many of the Silicon Valley plants. Although she loved the climate and the atmosphere of seething innovation in this corner of California near San Francisco, Frankie didn't care for the attendant secrecy and paranoia, where each innovator imagined that someone was out to steal his or her newest device. That was one reason why she'd begun consulting, working as often as she could out of her own house. Frankie didn't like being branded by a badge or stifled by corporate structure.

The receptionist had called the man in front of her Jules. It suited him somehow, conveying a faint flavor of creative bravado. She remembered that he hadn't been wearing a badge. Perhaps he was also contract help, hired on a temporary basis for the duration of a project.

He slowed down and she caught up with him, her arms a little strained from the weight of the terminal she carried. "Where are we taking this stuff, anyway?" His voice was pleasantly resonant, she thought, feeling an odd shiver go down her back. She wondered distractedly if she was getting sick. It wouldn't do to come down with something at the start of a fairly long project.

"Just a minute," she panted. "I have the office number on a piece of paper." Vainly she tried to fish the paper out of her back jeans pocket while still maintaining a grip on the bulky terminal. She couldn't manage it.

"If you turn around," the man called Jules said, wiggling the fingers of one hand while his horn-rims peeked over the top of the processor unit, "I'll see if I can get it."

With her back to him she couldn't see what he was doing. But she felt the brief warmth of his hand as he slid it into her pocket. Again that strange feeling quivered through her. *I hope it's not the flu,* she thought, twisting her head around. His fingers extracted the paper from her pocket and she took it from him. "Office number 128," she announced.

"Right down here." He strode a few feet farther and stopped in front of a door. "Even has a window. You must rate."

She pushed past him and set the terminal down on a desk, shaking out her arms with relief. "Just put 'em down anywhere," she told him, gesturing vaguely around. "I can move everything later if I need to."

He set down his load with alacrity and glanced curiously at the different parts of her system. She had gotten a kit from a well-known electronics company to build the terminal, but she'd put the processor together lovingly from her own design, housing it in a plain black chassis, the same as the disk drive.

"I know it's none of my business," he said, rubbing one hand though his thick curly thatch of hair, "but why are you bringing all this stuff here? Is someone going to buy it?"

Frankie gave him a pained look. "Certainly not. I built this system from the ground up—there isn't enough money anywhere to buy it. I'm planning to use it."

His eyebrows climbed up his forehead. "Maybe we should introduce ourselves. I'm Jules Jones."

Frankie nodded and stuck out her hand. "I gathered that from what the receptionist said. I'm Frankie Warburton."

Jules took her hand, his eyes fastened intently on her face. "Frankie Warburton! You're here to do the prototype work, aren't you? Were we not supposed to know that you're a woman?"

She shrugged, a little irritated. "Makes no difference to me. I don't usually put a note on the contract mentioning that I'm female. If the company is going to be concerned, maybe you should help me take my stuff right back to the car." He didn't answer immediately, so she nodded in satisfaction and pried the top of the processor off to get the cables she'd stored inside. "Who am I supposed to be working with on the prototype, anyway? Do you know? Must be somebody important if I have to work here so as to be available for consultation all the time." Her voice was faintly aggrieved. She much preferred her own sunny workroom at home to any office building, no matter how luxurious.

There was a stifled sound behind her, but when she looked back at Jules his face was perfectly sober. "One of those honchos, no doubt," he murmured. "Listen—give me your card. You *do* have a card, don't you?"

"Of course," she said, stung. "What do you want it for?" She reached into the faded blue jeans and pulled out a dog-eared card, passing it over to him when he put out his hand commandingly.

"Manure Man," he read. She felt her face flush, and grabbed for the card, but he held it tantalizingly out of reach. "The smell of success for your garden. Deliveries throughout the Bay area." He looked at her, his expression gently quizzical. "Do you moonlight?"

"Not my card," she muttered fiercely, finding the right piece of pasteboard and handing it over. She held out her own palm for the first card, and with a show of reluctance, he gave it back. "I'll need it for the roses," she explained.

He nodded and read her card, "V.F. Warburton, Ph.D. Microprocessing systems design." Then he asked, "What do the initials stand for?"

"*F* is for Frances," she told him, hoping it would be enough. "The softball team in grade school made it Frankie, and that was fine with me."

It wasn't enough. "So what's the *V* stand for?"

She didn't want to tell him. "Well...."

He smiled coaxingly. "Victoria? Vladimir?"

She realized breathlessly that she was going to tell him. "I'll give you a clue. I was born on February fourteenth."

"Valentine." He thought about it for a second, then gave her an all-encompassing look that started at her eyes and wandered down her body, making her nipples fire up. The heat washed through her face. She sat down. Luckily there was a chair underneath her. "I think it suits you."

She laughed shortly. Either he had less perception than she had credited him with, or he was shucking her. Valentine was a name that belonged with red satin and lace, with hearts and flowers. And she was a person for whom logic circuits were paramount, a person who designed computers and didn't quail at manure.

"And we have something in common," he continued politely. "I was born on Bastille Day, myself."

"Is that why they call you Jules?" Frankie opened the drawer of the desk at random, staring blindly at a pencil stub and some bent paper clips that inhabited the vast, dusty space.

"No, Jules came from an early fondness for Captain Nemo," he told her. Frankie barely heard him.

She definitely did not feel well. When Jules moved a little bit closer, holding out his hand and beginning to take leave of her, she felt tiny beads of perspiration break out along her forehead.

"Listen—" she heard herself saying with horror "—are you, er, busy tonight?"

The silence in the room was as heavy as the layer of clay under the topsoil in her garden. She had the panicky thought that he was married; her eyes rushed belatedly to his left hand and noted with relief the absence of a ring. She cleared her throat. "Maybe we could have dinner—you could give me the lowdown on the way they treat the help around here...." Her voice trailed off uneasily. For years she had received invitations such as the one she had just given, sometimes accepting, sometimes declining them. She hadn't realized the agony that could go into a casual-sounding request for a date. Unnerved by his silence, she finally brought herself to meet his glance.

His horn-rimmed glasses caught the light from the window, hiding the expression in his eyes. "I'd like that very much," he said gravely. He hesitated for a moment. "I did have something planned after dinner, but perhaps you'd care to go with me?"

She nodded dazedly. He accepted, she thought, thunderstruck. *I asked a man to go out to dinner, and he accepted!*

Jules glanced down at the card he still held in his hand. "Eight ninety-seven Wordsworth Avenue, Palo Alto," he read. "Is that your home address?" When she nodded, he smiled. "Sounds very poetic."

"I guess so," she mumbled blankly, still stupified with the unexpected turn of events. His smile faded a little.

"I'll pick you up at seven." He turned at the door, and once again she met his hazel eyes. She began to glow inside as if she'd swallowed a jigger of whisky neat. "Thanks for asking me, Valentine Frances Warburton."

Julian Jones walked away from office 128 shaking his head. He must have lost his mind once and for all, as his father always threatened he would. It wasn't like him to date a woman before knowing a lot about her—and her motives for going out with him. But there was something about Frankie that disarmed all suspicions of gold digging. In fact, he'd been ready to throw his habitual caution to the wind and ask her out when she'd taken the words right out of his mouth, fixing him with those anxious blue eyes, as blue as a twilit summer sky. "Not bad," he murmured to himself, repeating the bit of description. He took a little notebook out of his hip pocket and scribbled the poetic words in it.

He put the notebook away and continued down the hall to a corner-office suite, nodding affably to his secretary and going into the wood-paneled sanctum behind her. He sat in his chair, and put his feet up on the desk, heedless of the piles of paper that littered it. He'd never seen a woman with eyes so straightforward and honest.

He stretched his arms behind his head and allowed his thoughts to drift. Her hair, halfway between blond and brown, had been pulled back with a clip, but still fell almost to her waist. He had been tempted to touch the fine silky strands. Her face— he supposed it would be called heart shaped—was appropriate for someone named Valentine. He rubbed his forehead irritably, wondering why he felt so pleased at the thought that tonight he would doubtless get a chance to wind his fingers through her hair. He imagined how that slender, strong-looking body would feel if he held her in his arms...she hadn't been wearing a bra, that much was obvious.

His fingers tightened on the smooth leather of his chair, bringing the small pleasure shock that always swept through him when some chord in his sensitive, sensuous nature was touched. The fancy chair, the fancy office hadn't been his idea. It had been his father who felt that the dignity of Jones Morton, one of the leading semiconductor manufacturers in Silicon Valley, would be compromised by letting the vice-president for research stay in the shabby, comfortable office he'd had as a simple manager of R & D.

Jules preferred his old office but the new one wasn't bad—at least it was equal to Grif's. He felt his teeth clench, and with an effort relaxed them. He didn't mean to stew about Grif. Not until he had the prototype finished and working. Not until he could prove to his father that Jones Morton's entry into the field of electronic security was possible. Jeremiah Jones had been skeptical, and as president and chairman of the board, his skepticism translated into a firm veto. But Jules had gotten authorization to build a prototype—and he didn't mean to let the grass grow under his feet while he was working on it. So he'd hired a freelance designer to help. Enter Frankie Warburton.

The memory of her face seemed burned into his retinas. Strange. At first he'd hardly seen her, as if she'd had some kind of camouflage on. But when she'd asked him to carry in her computer—that face, those eyes, suddenly made an impact. He shook his head and told himself to get some perspective on the incident. She certainly wasn't the sleek, sophisticated kind of woman he normally dated. But then, he'd been finding women like that more trouble than they were worth for some time.

"It's great that she doesn't know who I am," he said aloud, bringing his feet to the floor and beginning to straighten the papers on his desk. "But she didn't seem to know who Wordsworth was either." He glanced down at Shakespeare's smiling, impervious face. "Good grief."

"You asked a man out for dinner?" Frankie winced at the raw incredulity in her roommate's voice. Sarabeth Connolly, thirty years old and a Texan by birth and inclination, generally spoke in a sweetly modulated drawl. She brought her leotard-clad legs down from the yoga headstand she'd been practicing and stared in stunned amazement at Frankie. "Honey child, are you sure you feel okay?"

Frankie slumped farther into the comfortable overstuffed chair and shrugged miserably. "Couple of times today I thought I was coming down with the flu. Maybe I was delirious."

Sarabeth laid a cool hand on her forehead. "No fever," she announced. "You were in your right mind, I reckon." Her lips began to twitch. "Well, aren't you going to get ready?"

Frankie closed her eyes. "Sarabeth," she said in despair, "this is a genuine, important dinner date! The last time I had this kind of date—well, things didn't go too well...." Her voice trailed off miserably.

Sarabeth sat cross-legged on the floor in front of Frankie's chair. "I know," she said, nodding solemnly. "You've gotten the idea somewhere that if a man shows he likes you, wants to get to know you better, he's going to be too much trouble to handle." She paused thoughtfully. "That attitude may simplify life, but it surely does make things dull. It makes you seem remote or something. Then coming on to you becomes a challenge for jerks like Fred Metzger."

Frankie shuddered and put a hand over her face. "Don't remind me! He was so *damp*—damp hands, wet lips—ugh!" She sat up straighter. "But of course, I only went out with him because he pestered me so. Things won't be like that with Jules."

"At least the shoe will be on the other foot this time," Sarabeth agreed. "Maybe you'll be the one with damp palms."

"Why, Sarabeth Connolly!" Frankie bounced in the chair with indignation. "What a thing to wish on your roommate and business associate. May all your programs be lost in a power failure." She gnawed her lip. "I'm treating this whole thing far too importantly," she muttered. "I act like I've never had a boyfriend before or something. What's the matter with me? Just last week I went to the Giants' opener with what's his name."

Sarabeth smiled. "He made a big impression, I can see." She lifted her legs toward the ceiling again. Her voice sounded oddly muffled coming from down near the floor. "You've never cared about any of the men you date sufficiently to get into this kind of state over them," she pointed out in calm, didactic tones. "Even that guy you had the affair with—Gary something, wasn't it? It's my belief you were just using the poor critter to find out about sex. Once you had it down pat, you lost interest—in it and him."

"Sarabeth!" This time Frankie was out of the chair as if it had a manual ejection mode. "That's the cruelest thing you could possibly say," she stammered heatedly. "You make me sound callous and shallow and self-centered...."

Sarabeth came out of the headstand and rested prone on the floor for a minute. "I didn't mean to rile you," she said placatingly. "After all, honey, we're all like that to a certain extent. But if you'd been in love with the guy, you wouldn't have just written him off so casually, now would you?"

"Oh, love," Frankie said scornfully. "Phooey on it! You know what I think about that particular figment of imagination. If love were possible, I would have felt it for Gary. I thought I *did* feel it, in fact, until he had to go away on business for a couple of weeks and I didn't even miss him. Love is an illusion, an excuse we humans have thought up for playing footsie. In my investigations—"

Sarabeth's snort of laughter brought her up short. "Okay," she said, glaring at her roommate, "I admit that I have, after a fashion, done some research on the topics of love and passion. Naturally I found it difficult to use the scientific method while conducting my experiments. But I did try to be impartial."

Sarabeth was grinning openly, and Frankie found it hard to maintain her air of injured innocence. "And your results, professor?"

"I found," Frankie said with a grand gesture, "that what we call love is really just a confusing mass of hormonal emotion, which is individual to each person. I will grant that passion exists, especially in men—"

"Especially in Fred Metzger," Sarabeth put in. Frankie ignored the interruption with lofty unconcern.

"But as for love, I cannot find any concrete evi-

dence of its existence—'' She broke off and looked
at Sarabeth soberly. "That's why I didn't continue
the affair with Gary. Actually, you're probably
right. Deep down, I think I felt it was time I discovered what sex was like. When I realized that's
all I was doing, I couldn't go on. And I think he
was just as relieved as I was to call it quits. I must
have been a pretty cold fish in bed.'' She stared
down at the frayed laces of her sneakers. "What an
idiot I was to ask Jules out! I should stick to computers and forget about men.''

Sarabeth looked at her sharply. "Don't be silly,
girl. The fact that you asked him out is proof that
there's hope for you.'' She thought for a moment.
"A little romance might do you a world of good.
You haven't dated anyone seriously since you
broke up with Gary. Hey, was he good in bed?''

Frankie responded to the humor in Sarabeth's
grin. "How should I know?'' A wry smile lifted the
corners of her mouth. "I don't have sufficient data
to make a comparison.''

"Is that why you asked Jules for a date?''

Startled into action, Frankie swung around,
whacking her funny bone on the back of the chair.
"Of course not!'' She rubbed her throbbing elbow,
avoiding Sarabeth's knowing look. "I tell you, I
don't know why I asked him out. The words
just...just came out of my mouth!''

"Just came out of your mouth,'' Sarabeth repeated annoyingly. "Of course. Well, you must
have had some reason, however buried it is. It's my
belief the old hormones were calling.''

"Don't be silly!'' Frankie looked at the clock and
ran for the shower. While she soaped and rinsed,
Sarabeth's words stayed with her. She found her
hands lingering on the gentle slopes of her breasts.

Hastily she climbed out of the shower and toweled off.

Whether Sarabeth was right or not, when Frankie went to her closet for fresh clothes, her hand went unerringly to the hanger with the black silk jump suit on it. She was zipping it up when Sarabeth came into the room, ready for her own date that evening.

"Whew!" Sarabeth's eyebrows went up as she took in the sleek lines of the jump suit. "Where did you get that? I've never seen you in anything but jeans or that gray flannel business suit."

Frankie's hand hovered indecisively over the zipper, finally leaving it open a couple of inches at the throat. "My mother sent it." She echoed Sarabeth's smile with a grin of her own. "I guess it does seem funny for anyone's mother to send them *this*." Seeing how the jump suit molded itself to her body, she had to laugh. "But mother's getting desperate. No wedding pictures to show the bridge club, no baby on a bearskin rug."

Sarabeth laughed too. "You know how they say women have a biological clock that urges them to have children? Maybe your mother has one that's set for grandchildren." She eyed Frankie critically and whisked the zipper down four more inches. "Don't be chicken. If you're going to wear something like that, you've got to do it right. Show a little skin."

"I think mother would rather I got married before having the grandchildren," Frankie protested, bringing the zipper up two inches. "I don't want to catch cold."

"What are you going to do with your hair?" Sarabeth flicked her own shiny, perfectly arranged, pale gold hair.

"Do with it?" Frankie felt insecurity welling up inside her. "Do I have to do something with it?"

Sarabeth ignored her. "You could do it in a kind of pompadour...." She stood behind Frankie, gathering her hair, twisting, using a large ebony hair slide from the dresser top to secure it. "There. Sexy but dignified." The doorbell rang and she glanced at her watch. "That will be Desmond. I have to go. Have a good time and don't worry—I'll be back very late, if at all, so the coast is clear!" With a final knowing smile she was gone.

Alone, Frankie stared at the image in her mirror. With her hair making a gentle frame around her face, its fine-boned contours became more obvious. Moving dreamily, she splashed on some of the rose essence she'd made the year before. Her one tube of mascara was dried up, so she borrowed some from Sarabeth's dresser, enjoying the difference it made when her long sandy lashes were darkened. For a moment she flirted with the idea of nail polish, then pulled herself up sternly. There was no point in going overboard, after all. She had long since observed that nail polish flaked and chipped too soon after application to make it a time- and cost-effective method of grooming.

She took one more look in the full-length mirror. Freed from her usual uniform of jeans and T-shirt, her body in the black silk flared with womanly fullness at breast and hip. She felt sophisticated and soft—a novel experience. When the doorbell rang again she went to answer it, confident and terrified at the same time.

Jules no longer wore Shakespeare's face on his chest. Instead he had on a crisp white open-throated shirt under a navy blazer and well-cut tan trousers. His eyes widened when he saw her.

"You're ready, then," he said, taking her hand in an impulsive gesture and bending to brush his lips over the back. This time when she felt the strange sensation, she knew what it was. Sarabeth was right. It was hormones—and it was powerful!

She snatched her hand away as if it burned. Jules looked quizzically at her. "Shall we be going then?" she blurted, looking around agitatedly. She picked up the big leather pouch that served as her handbag, realizing too late that she should have found something small and dainty among Sarabeth's plentiful collection. But it wasn't important. She stepped out and locked the door, joining Jules on the porch.

Frankie's house was one of the bungalows that abounded in Palo Alto on quiet tree-lined streets. When she and Sarabeth had decided to free lance together, Frankie handling hardware requests and Sarabeth writing the software, Sarabeth had moved in to help her make the house payments during those first perilous, uncertain months of being on their own.

Now, when their reputations for thoroughness and professionalism made their financial positions secure, Sarabeth could have afforded her own house, and Frankie could have made the payments alone. But they enjoyed each other's undemanding companionship and the arrangement stayed. Sarabeth took care of most of the inside housework, and Frankie did the outside.

The fruits—or scents—of her labors were palpable as soon as they stepped outside. The porch was shaded by thick cables of wisteria that dangled graceful purple flowers. Rose trees paraded down either side of the front walk, flanked by beds crowded with foxglove, nasturtium, lilies and irises. The early-May evening was filled with the dizzying fragrances of the flowers.

Jules inhaled appreciatively. "I don't detect any traces of Manure Man," he remarked as he followed Frankie to the front gate. "Are you responsible for all these flowers?"

Frankie nodded, wondering if she should offer to drive. Before she could speak Jules was ushering her into his car. Instead of the Morris, he drove a twenty-year-old Jaguar in immaculate condition. "It's a healthy hobby," she said, running a hand over the smooth leather of the seat. "Do you restore cars in your spare time?"

He glanced at her. "That's one of the things I do in my spare time. Where are we going?"

She blinked, and he repeated his question patiently. "You did invite me, didn't you? I assumed—"

"Yes, of course," she said hurriedly. "I should have picked you up, I guess." She directed him to an intimate little restaurant in downtown Palo Alto, feeling the uncertainty in her crowd out the tenuous sophistication that had pervaded her earlier. What was the matter with her, asking out a man as suave and as charming as Jules? Now that she saw him away from the office setting where she'd met most of the men she knew, she realized he was probably used to accompanying sleek, svelte women of the world. Maybe because she'd asked him out, he'd gotten the idea that this was all routine to her. She gulped nervously. The silence seemed labored, but she was suddenly incapable of opening her mouth.

Jules found a place to park near the restaurant, but he didn't open his car door immediately. He turned to Frankie, reaching tentative fingers to touch her hair. "You look different with your hair up," he murmured. He traced the outline of her lips, and she tried to keep from showing how the graze of his fingers burned.

His hand went under her chin. "Why don't we just get this out of the way?" His voice grew tender as his lips approached hers. As their mouths touched, she closed her eyes, feeling an unbearable sweetness flood her body. His lips were soft, like rose petals, but electrifying. Her lips trembled beneath his. When he took his mouth away she stared up at him, still tasting the sweetness of his kiss.

Jules felt enmeshed by the expression in her eyes, the bemusement, the desire for him so inadequately concealed. At last she whispered, "What was that for?"

For keeps, he wanted to say. The impulse to utter such words frightened him. He cleared his throat and put a little space between them. He wanted to make a flippant remark, something to put the evening back into the realm of casual dating, but found himself telling her the truth. "I didn't want to spend all evening wondering when I was going to kiss you. Now the suspense is over."

Something sparked briefly in her eyes—was it anger? She turned away and said, prosaically enough, "Was a kiss such a foregone conclusion?"

His hands went to her shoulders, pulling her around to face him again. "Between us," he told her, feeling the words spill out of him without volition, "a lot more than a kiss is foregone." He hesitated, surprised at his own vehemence but unable to stem his words. "We're going to be friends—and more than friends. Let's not play games with each other."

For a moment she seemed to resist. Then her

shoulders relaxed under his hands and she looked at him again. Her eyes had an artless clarity and he felt afraid to delve too thoroughly into what they seemed to be telling him. "I don't know how to play games...not those kinds," she said gruffly. "I—I'm handicapped by the fact I can't play."

Laughter bubbled up inside him. "Lady, you don't seem handicapped to me, but I'll bear it in mind." He let go of her reluctantly. "I'm starving. Why are we sitting here when food waits for us somewhere else?"

Her chuckle had a delightfully spontaneous sound. "By all means, let's eat. It was dinner I asked you out for, after all, not just conversation." An impish smile showed unexpected dimples. God, he thought, *I'm going to be besotted any minute now.* "And you do mean to sing for your supper by telling me how to keep my nose clean at Jones Morton, don't you?" She opened her car door and he vaulted out of his seat to join her.

"Right," he said hazily, taking her arm and beaming down at her. "Anything you say."

The restaurant was one that Sarabeth had mentioned as having both good food and a nice ambience. She had neglected to mention that the maître d' would be wearing a tuxedo. Frankie sat in the chair that this extremely correct individual pulled out for her and raised her eyebrows at Jules. After the stiff black back had receded, she leaned across the table to whisper, "My, he's grand, isn't he?"

His lips quirked as he opened his menu. "What did you expect? This is a very nice restaurant."

"Oh, dear. Maybe we should have gone to Taco Bell." She opened her own menu and looked at it in dismay. "There are no prices in here! How will I know if your order is going to bankrupt me?"

He looked faintly taken aback. "I've got prices. I didn't realize they still left them off women's menus."

Frankie traded menus with him. "I hope you remember which are the inexpensive items." He shot a startled look at her, then burst into laughter as he saw her dancing eyes.

"Miss Warburton, you are an original!" For a moment they perused the menu in silence, but when the waiter materialized and Frankie grandly told him that the gentleman was her guest and would he please bestow the check accordingly, Jules laughed again.

After that the evening seemed to pass in a blur of delight for Frankie. The rapport she and Jules had established in the car flowed on through the meal, making conversation easy, sparkling. She felt witty and attractive, not at all like the usual Frankie Warburton. They ate melon and prosciutto, scampi and tiny perfectly cooked medallions of veal. Once, after a particularly gratifying response from Jules to an irreverent comment of hers, she clapped her hands to her face and stared at him. "My God," she breathed, "I'm flirting!"

"You are?" He paused and smiled. "Whatever it is you're doing, don't stop. I adore it."

Confused, she felt hot color wash up her neck. Something intent in his gaze threw her out of her stride for a moment. *He's flirting too,* she told herself, the thought somewhat sobering. But then he took her hand, pressing it urgently. "Frankie? What did I say? Don't look like that!" His expression melted her.

"I was just thinking...why didn't anyone tell me how much fun flirting is?" He shouted with laughter and her spirits lifted again.

After dinner he took her to an art gallery where a new show was opening. They walked the few blocks to the place, talking intently, still wrapped in the warmth of their accord. Somehow she was not surprised to find that several charming watercolor landscapes had been painted by Jules. He accepted her compliments with casual aplomb. "I enjoy it," he said, shrugging, "but I'm not *dedicated* to it. I'm a dilettante, I guess you'd say."

Frankie felt well fed, smooth with contentment. She glanced around the room. The gallery was full of well-dressed people talking at the tops of their lungs, but the noise and glitter were somehow at a distance, as if she and Jules were alone in an iridescent bubble of affinity.

That illusion was destroyed in two minutes when a perfectly dressed young man accosted them. He bestowed a thin-lipped smile between Jules and Frankie, giving Jules a languid handshake. "Great pictures," he said carelessly. "Beats me how you find time to do them." His eyes swept Frankie in a cold appraisal devoid of any friendly overtones. "Who's this, Jules?" He held out his hand to Frankie; she was surprised at her reluctance to shake it. "I'm Grif Morton. Jules is like a brother to me, aren't you, old man?"

Suddenly the names clicked. Frankie stared from Jules's forbidding frown to the younger man's watchful pose. "Jones," she whispered, stricken, "and Morton. How could I have been so stupid?"

2

JULES DROVE WITHOUT SPEAKING, the stern lines of his face made even harsher by the eerie glow of the dashboard lights. Frankie watched him uneasily. He'd hauled her out of the art gallery as if staying one more minute near Grif Morton would have stifled him. It was obvious he was angry; she just didn't know why. After all, she was the one who'd been made to look like a fool. "Why didn't you tell me?" Her voice sounded loud and raw in the heavy quiet.

He flicked a glance at her and returned his attention to the road. "I enjoyed the novelty of being just a regular guy," he said dryly. "Would you have asked me out if you'd known I was Julian Jones, son of one of Jones Morton's founders?"

Frankie shook her head, then chewed uncertainly on her lip. "I don't think so, but I don't know for sure." A shaky laugh escaped her. "I've never asked a man out before—I was floored when the words came out of my mouth. I could have been just stupid enough...."

Her voice trailed off and Jules filled in for her grimly. "Just stupid enough to ask the boss's son out? Why would that have been so dumb?"

"You know why," she whispered.

Jules stopped the car in front of her house and turned to her, taking her into his arms with a swiftness that forestalled any attempt she could have made to escape. "Because of this?" His lips came down on hers, no longer soft and questing as they had been earlier.

This time the kiss was a demand, a fierce outpouring of the sexual tension that had simmered between them all evening. For once Frankie was unable to summon logic to her defense. All she could think of was getting more—more of the sweetness, more of the fire that blazed up in her when he moved his lips on hers, asking, taking.

When his tongue sought out hers, she had no thought of denying the velvety combat that ensued. Dimly she realized that she had both hands in his thick curly hair, clutching as if desperate for an anchor. Their hot breaths mingled as they strove for air. When his hands moved up her sides to rest beneath the full weight of her breasts, she shuddered with longing.

He took her response for acquiescence, bringing his palms around to cup her roundness. Her breasts were taut, aching for his touch. His hand lingered along the slopes before slipping inside the silken fabric to find her wildly beating heart.

She nearly sobbed with relief when his tormenting fingers finally touched one hard thrusting nipple, circling with maddening deliberation. She panted desirous words into his mouth, her breast heaving against his hand. He groaned and gathered her to him, pressing as much of their bodies together as was possible in the confines of the car. The gearshift knob dug painfully into the flesh of her left thigh, and she felt Jules grunt as his ribs met the steering wheel.

Reluctantly he released her. "I think I got carried away." He took off his horn-rims and cleaned them with his handkerchief. "You fogged up my glasses, woman." When she didn't reply, his voice softened. "I'm sorry, Frankie. I didn't mean to get so rambunctious."

She stared up at him, her mouth suddenly dry. She wanted him—wanted him more than she'd ever imagined could be possible. She had thought her rather prosaic experience with Gary was the height of passion; after it was over, she had felt a rational disdain for her friends who were helplessly caught in the grip of fierce physical sensations. Now she realized that it might be impossible to deny them.

She felt compelled to ask Jules in for a drink. But if she asked him in, she was as good as inviting more of what had just happened. And what had just occurred usually had only one conclusion. Did she want to make love with him? The picture that thought created in her mind brought an intoxicating rush of feeling. She licked her lips. Her voice came out in a hoarse whisper. "Why—why don't you come in for a nightcap, Jules?"

He kissed her once more, his lips a quick hard blaze against hers, then pushed her gently away. "Thanks. I'd like that." With a ragged smile he leaned across her and opened the car door.

He took her hand as they moved up the walk, through the fragrance of roses mingled with the sweetness of orange blossom. His palm was hard and warm against hers. She got the key in the lock on the third try, not helped by the way he wrapped his arms around her and pressed their bodies together with heady intimacy.

She ushered him into the small cozy living room. In the mirror that hung over the fireplace she caught a glimpse of him, his lean strength belied by the innocuous horn-rims. Standing beside him was

a slight, wild-haired woman—herself! "Excuse me
for a minute," she mumbled. "Gotta go... bathroom... help yourself to some brandy." She pointed to one of the glass-fronted bookcases on either
side of the fireplace, where a brandy decanter and
some snifters occupied one shelf, and fled.

In the bathroom she took the ebony hair slide out
of her hair, letting the tumbled mass fall down her
back. There was no use trying to duplicate the effect Sarabeth had achieved with so little effort. The
subtleties of hairstyle were a total mystery to
Frankie. Raising her arm to brush her hair, she
noticed how her breasts strained against the black
silk as if pleading for touch. She studied her reflection in the mirror for a moment, then grinned
recklessly at herself and lowered the zipper another
two inches. "Let's hear it for the hormones," she
said under her breath, and went out to the living
room.

Two snifters of brandy waited on the sleek glass
coffee table. Jules was reading the titles of the books
through the leaded bookcase doors. She stood for a
moment looking at his broad back in the well-cut
navy blazer, the way his hair curled just over his
collar, the studious look of the horn-rims belying
the impression of power and control, and she was
struck by a sudden frightening sense of inevitabil-
ity regarding him.

Until that night her life had been uncomplicated,
full of absorbing work and easy friendships. Now
something told her that had come to an end. She
felt changed, transmuted. She had always taken
pride in her strong female body, but at the moment
she realized that some hidden, dormant part of her
was more than female—it was feminine, with in-
stincts and reactions that made her long to be al-

luring, sexy, flirtatious. Suddenly, because of Jules, everything seemed turned upside down—difficult instead of comfortable, anxious instead of relaxed. Then he turned and saw her, and her fears were submerged in the rush of excitement his look generated.

Frankie crossed the room for the snifter Jules held out, her eyes still riveted on his. He lifted his glass and she raised hers to touch it. "I don't know if it's gauche to toast with brandy," he said huskily, his eyes holding hers intently, "but I'd like to pledge you, Valentine Frances Warburton—a woman like no other I've ever known." She stared at him wide-eyed, made solemn for a moment by his expression. He held back nothing of the heat that kindled between them. She gulped the brandy, welcoming its steadying flame.

Jules took the glass from her hand and set it gently on the coffee table with his own. As he straightened, he removed the horn-rims, and she saw with dreamy acuity that his eyes were a pleasing shade of brown green. He put the glasses absently in his jacket pocket, fixing her with that bone-shaking look of devouring hunger.

Frankie didn't remember moving. But suddenly they were kissing fervently, their lips and tongues creating moist urgent fire. His hands stroked her sleek curves as if every touch was more impossibly pleasurable than the one before. She indulged her own fingers by sliding her hands under his jacket, along the waistband of his pants, pulling his shirt out to reach the supple flesh beneath. His growl of gratification was accompanied by a surge of motion that ended somehow with the two of them flat on the couch.

Their mouths met again and again, clinging,

parting, joining. With delicate touches of lips and tongue he explored the contour of her mouth, making her gasp at the sudden shaft of desire as he licked at her lower lip, finding and sipping the sweet honey of passion. She arched longingly against him and he filled his hands with her breasts, plucking the taut peaks beneath the black silk to full arousal. Their bodies fought to find every possible way to touch, until his lean frame pressed her back into the corner of the couch. He found the zipper of the jump suit and brought it down to her waist, pushing the fabric off her skin with hot impatient hands. She felt her desires spiral out of control as his hands pleasured her breasts. When he straightened she nearly cried out for the loss of it.

His eyes swept the length of her and grew passion heavy as he looked at her, with hair tumbled around her, breasts gleaming naked. He closed his eyes briefly. "You are so beautiful." His voice was thick and rasped along her nerve endings like an exquisite pain. He put one hand around her neck under her hair and pulled her up for his kiss. "Without my glasses," he whispered in her ear while the other hand opened the jump suit farther, "I can't see too well. Have to look at things...very close up...." His mouth trailed down her neck and fastened on a nipple while his fingers moved down the curve of her hip, tantalizing newly discovered territory there.

She began to feel a restless, melting fever that brought continuous moans from the back of her throat. Her hands wandered over the sleek planes of his back, while her legs, shifting uncontrollably, encountered the hard core of his need. He surged against her, a tremor shaking him as he held her tightly. "My God, lady—" Their lips met again, fusing all the blazing caresses into one dark velvet endless free-fall of spiraling sensuality.

He pulled his mouth away with a desperate groan. "I want to make love to you." The husky note in his voice made her open her eyes; what she saw in his molten gaze made her shut them again blissfully. But his words woke her to the reality of their actions, and she thought, *We've only known each other since this morning.*

"It's too soon," she said, stupidly, unable to find the words to articulate her fear that he would think her cheap, easy, used to passions soon ignited— and soon over.

"Frankie." The urgency in his voice made her open her eyes again. He cupped her face in his warm rough palms, his gaze devouring her. "I can't argue with you over the number of hours we've known each other. But this...this is apart from time." He hesitated, his eyes searching hers. Then he kissed her with indescribable tenderness. "Something in me has always known you, I think," he whispered.

For a long moment they stared at each other. Then, shuddering, Frankie turned her face away. "I understand what you're saying, Jules." She spoke the words reluctantly but with finality. "I just don't...don't know what to make of all this. It's... I'm confused and I need some time to think, and we need to know more about each other...."

Jules stared down at her, his eyes glittering with unexpressed emotion. At last he took a deep breath and stood beside the couch. "Right," he said crisply. "What you say is true." Without his body warm and vital against hers, Frankie felt the cold draft make gooseflesh on her chest. She groped for the zipper on her jump suit just as Jules bent to swing her up into his arms. "Which way is the bedroom?"

"Jules," she said, gasping as he staggered a couple of steps. "Put me down! I thought you said—I told you—"

"I'm not going to force myself on you or anything," he told her, panting slightly. "You want us to get to know each other. Fine by me. We'll be friends, right?" He didn't wait for her reply. "Right. And as a friend, I feel the least I can do is help you into your jammies, turn down your bed, find out what color your toothbrush is—"

He carried her out of the living room as he spoke. By this time she was laughing, clinging helplessly with her arms around his neck. "I'm too heavy," she protested. He cannoned off the doorframe and lurched into the hall. "Ouch! If I don't break your back, you'll probably break mine!"

"Don't talk so much. Hold your breath and you'll be lighter," he grunted, turning into Sarabeth's room. He stood for a moment in the doorway, then backed cautiously out. "Wrong room."

"Astute." Frankie raised her eyebrows at him, trying to make her body small when she saw him aiming at the door to her bedroom. He dropped her on her bed and she lay there in a swirl of silky brown hair, laughing up at him. "How did you know which one was mine?"

His eyes kindled as he looked at her and she felt her skin prickle into tingling awareness. He crouched over her on the bed, not touching her, but imprisoning her body with his arms and legs. "Wasn't hard," he growled thickly. "You wouldn't have the kind of furniture where everything matches." With one hand he began gently

stripping off her jump suit. The brush of his fingers
was light, tantalizing torture.

"Look, Jules," she said, trying to summon the
willpower to resist, "I can do it myself, you know."

"Of course you can," he murmured soothingly.
"But I've already started." He freed her arms and
began to push the fabric off her hips. "Might as
well let me finish."

"Jules—" They were both having trouble breathing, she noticed vaguely. "Jules, maybe what I said
in the living room. Maybe I was wrong. Oh, Jules!"
The jump suit lay in a puddle on the floor beside the
bed, and his hands were moving slowly up her legs
toward her sole remaining garment, practical white
cotton underpants. She quivered as he slid his
fingers under the elastic. Then his hands stopped.
"Jules?"

They looked at each other with helpless desire.
"No," Jules said at last. "No, you weren't wrong,
and we both know it." He turned away with an
abrupt movement and rooted under her pillow.
"Ah, a real traditionalist. Keep your nighty where
your mother told you to." He held up her striped
jersey nightshirt and tugged it over her head,
pulling it down ruthlessly over her breasts and
hips, pulling her to her feet finally and holding her
close.

She melted into his arms, already dreading the
moment when he would leave. "Jules," she whispered achingly. "I think I want you to stay."

He kissed her with lingering thoroughness. "I
couldn't stay unless we made love, and you're
right, we need time to get to know each other. Besides," he added, laughter in his voice, "I wasn't
expecting this to happen, and I didn't bring any—
protection. Do you have...?" He watched her ex-

pression of puzzlement change into sudden comprehension. A blush flooded her face as she shook her head. "I didn't think so." There was satisfaction in his voice. She must not be seeing any other men, and that pleased him. "Next time we get carried away, we'll be prepared."

Frankie looked up into his face wonderingly. "You really are the most—" she began, then shrugged helplessly. "I think maybe I'm an idiot to let you get away tonight. Some smarter woman is going to snabble you off when you walk out the door, and I'll kick myself forever for not keeping you here."

The laughter died in his eyes. "No," he whispered harshly. "You won't escape so easily. This—what's happening to us—doesn't come that often. I'm not letting it get away."

"What?" The intensity of his words stirred the hair on the back of her neck. "What are you talking about?"

He let go of her and strode to the door of her bedroom, looking back as he paused there with a devilish smile. "I'm talking about love, my Valentine. Love at first date. See you in the morning. We'll have a meeting first thing."

It took a moment for his words to penetrate, another moment for her body to obey her commands to move. When she reached the living-room door he had already let himself out. She flew to the window and saw the Jaguar pull smoothly away from the curb. "Just a minute, Jules Jones," she cried, finding her voice at last. "Just hold on! I don't believe in love!" Her words echoed hollowly in the empty living room and she looked around, dazed. She had met a man at work this morning, gone to dinner with him this evening, exchanged passionate embraces with him afterward—and now she was standing in the living room in her nightshirt, shouting into a void. If it hadn't been for the two empty brandy snifters on the coffee table, she might have believed it all to be a dream.

She picked up the snifters and carried them slowly into the kitchen. "None of this really happened," she muttered to herself. "I'll go into work tomorrow and set Jules straight about this love business. He'll look at me like I've lost my mind and then he'll make some excuse to leave the room and the loony bin men will come and take me away...." Stifling a yawn she finished her nighttime ritual and climbed into her big old wrought-iron bed. She had snuggled into her pillow when a disquieting thought hit her. He'd said they'd have a meeting first thing. Was Jules the honcho she would be working with on the prototype?

Frankie sat up, her hand going to the light switch. She thought about calling Jules to clarify the situation, then shrugged and lay back down again. It would have been smart to find out if they were going to be involved closely at work before letting herself lose all control like she had on the living-room couch. But she was too tired tonight to grapple with the problems she could see looming ahead. Something would work out.

Just before unconsciousness took her she felt the corners of her mouth lift. Crazy Jules, she thought with drowsy pleasure.

3

FRANKIE STOOD at the bulletin board outside her office door sipping coffee from her big white mug. The board was covered with three by five-inch cards advertising computer equipment, cars, stereos and health-club memberships for sale, with a sprinkling of posters promoting community events and Jones Morton activities. Attention, Poets! proclaimed one tattered sheet of mimeograph paper. Next to it was a sheet announcing the Research and Development Division Picnic and Barbecue at Foothill Park. Idly Frankie noticed that the picnic was next week; perhaps she would go—if she was still working on the prototype by then.

She took another sip of coffee. Behind her, through the open door of her office, her equipment hummed steadily. She had gotten to Jones Morton early that morning, wandering through the various departments to the one housing Research and Development and her temporary office. She felt an odd combination of nervousness and exhilaration at the thought of seeing Jules again, especially since she now knew he was her boss.

There had been a note from him on her desk when she'd gotten in, telling her that they'd be working together and that his secretary was holding the printed circuit layouts for the electronic security prototype. She'd picked them up and looked over them, expecting every five minutes to see Jules's love-stricken face.

But the quelling speech she'd planned remained undelivered—Jules evidently didn't work conventional office hours. Finally she'd wandered into the reception area for a cup of coffee. Nan had pounced gleefully on her with a security badge, which was clipped to the V-neck of her turquoise polo shirt. Frankie glanced down at it for a second in frowning dislike. She felt like a heifer who'd just been branded.

Her reverie was interrupted by a faintly familiar voice, so cold and expressionless it sent a ripple of disquiet down her back. "Well, Ms Warburton. I didn't realize you were a Jones Morton employee when I met you last night. You work with Jules?"

Frankie glanced up and saw Grif Morton standing next to her at the bulletin board. His expression was the same chillingly polite one he'd worn at the art gallery the night before, but she felt more speculation in his look.

"Good morning, Mr. Morton." Her voice was cool, covering up an unexpected nervousness. "I've been hired on temporarily as contract help." She took another sip of coffee and fixed her attention once more on the bulletin board. "Multibus system," one of the cards read. "IEEE compatible. Call extension 293 with best offer."

"Please, not so formal." His mouth relaxed enough to let a tight smile through. "Call me Grif." His eyes traveled once up and down her, with no apparent feeling involved. "I take it you're working on Jules's new little project?"

"Yes."

"What do you think of it?"

The abrupt question made her blink. Reacting to the intentness in his voice, she hedged. "I've hardly had time to look at it yet," she said, inching toward her office door.

Grif watched her go, raising one eyebrow. "Good old Jules," he murmured. "Always trying to come up with something innovative. Occasionally he even succeeds." His voice was mild, but the ice ran deep in it. Not knowing how to reply, Frankie maintained a discreet silence as she edged into her office.

Grif followed her, standing rigid in the doorway, his eyes darting over the printed circuit layouts she'd left unrolled on her desk. The sudden sharpening of his gaze made Frankie move casually to roll up the sheets of vellum. She perched on her desk and returned Grif's stare. He wasn't much above medium height, with sandy hair and pale gray eyes above a sharp, knife-blade nose. His trousers were perfectly creased, his shirt beautifully ironed, his tie just the right combination of dash and conservatism. Frankie decided that she disliked him very much.

"So this is your famous system." She narrowed her eyes. He had pretended not to know who she was, but he'd known somehow about her system. Without waiting for an invitation he moved through the door toward her computer. "I heard some of the engineers in the cafeteria yesterday talking about it. They said you've got just about every kind of microprocessor that exists tucked into the backplane. Is that true?"

He reached for the top of the processor unit, but Frankie moved in front of him before he could touch it. "The system's running," she pointed out. "I prefer that you don't poke around while it's turned on." She smiled sweetly at him. "You might get a shock."

"I see." His eyes narrowed. "You know, my dear—"

"Warburton."

"What?" She'd thrown him off stride temporarily.

"You can call me Ms Warburton." The animosity she felt for him filtered into her voice. He spoke to her directly, with cold finality.

"You and Jules may be very close, Ms Warburton." The way he said her name was an insult. "But I don't know if he's told you how things operate here at Jones Morton. You see, his father, Jeremiah, is the Jones half. But since my father is no longer active in the business, *I* am the Morton half. If you want to keep this contract, you'll stay on my good side." He made another one of his dispassionate surveys of her person. "You know, Jules is notorious for his temporary enthusiasms—both at work and in bed." She felt the hot blood rise in her face and bit her tongue to keep an angry retort at bay. She could tell he enjoyed knowing that he'd struck a nerve. "But I'm more tenacious in my approach. Those who work for me and with me know that I reward loyalty. You might want to think about that." He waited for a moment, but Frankie could find nothing to say. She stared back at him, trying to keep the uneasiness he aroused in her out of her face. "Just in case Jules's little project goes down the drain. His projects often do, you know."

Frankie prevented herself with an effort from grinding her teeth in fear and rage. "If you're finished," she said, striving to keep her voice even and icy, and not quite succeeding, "I have some work to do, Mr. Morton." She took hold of the doorknob pointedly, and after one more cold smile, Grif Morton went.

With a sigh of relief she shut the door after him. She sank into the desk chair and realized she was shaking. Such disturbing encounters hadn't often come her way. *At least I didn't just gibber senselessly at him,* she thought. Now that Grif Morton was gone, several clever cutting things she should have said leaped into her mind. "If he'd been a snake, he'd have bitten me," she said aloud just as the door opened again. She whirled in her chair, but it was Jules and not Grif. "Thank goodness."

Jules stood in the doorway as Grif had done, but there the resemblance ended. His hair was damp and curly from a shower, his eyes warm and smiling behind his glasses. The rugby shirt he wore did nothing to disguise the smooth muscles of his chest; his clean but faded jeans clung to slim hips and thighs. Frankie closed her eyes for a moment. He looked fine—too fine. She felt the fires of desire begin to simmer.

"You look good in the morning," he murmured, a seductive note in his deep voice.

"It's practically afternoon already," Frankie snapped, trying to collect her thoughts. There was something she meant to say. Bemused, she stared up at Jules until he sat on the desk in front of her. He put out one finger to trace the line of her nose.

"Don't exaggerate." His lazy smile deepened as he touched her mouth and felt the involuntary shudder ripple through her. "It's only ten o'clock. I see you got the PC layouts okay. I forgot to tell you last night we would be working together. Had something else on my mind." He watched her blush with a knowing grin. "Did you miss me this morning?"

Frankie moved a little away and licked her lips. "I would have had time to miss you, seeing how late you come to work," she said, searching for a diversion. "But as it happens, I've been quite well entertained by your childhood buddy, Grif Morton."

Jules stiffened, the warmth vanishing from his face. "Grif? What did he want?"

Shrugging, Frankie kept her eyes on Jules. There was something going on that she didn't understand yet, and she meant to dig it out. "He was interested in your prototype. And for some strange reason, he wanted me to know that he rewards loyalty."

Jules seized on the first part of her sentence. "What did you tell him? Did you let him see the PC layouts?" His voice was tense. Frankie stared at him, puzzled.

"As a matter of fact, I didn't like his cold-fish act, so I rolled the layouts up before he could get a good look. What's going on between you two, anyway?"

Jules didn't answer for a moment. He stood up, his hands clenched, his face set in frowning lines. Then he looked at Frankie. For a moment he seemed to be measuring her, so piercing and impersonal was his gaze. Then, as if making up his mind, he put his hands on her shoulders. The warm current generated by his touch feathered through her. She forced her thoughts into a more seemly path.

"Grif wants to know about my project so he can sabotage it," Jules said, his eyes still hard on her face. She let the words sink in, unable to accept their import. When she didn't reply at once, Jules went on, his calm unemotional voice belied by the harshness of his face. "Perhaps he mentioned that most of my projects lately have come to no good end. Sometimes the prototype fails when I'm demonstrating it in the preproduction trials. Or sometimes I can't even get a prototype put together because the specifications have mysteriously changed. Needless to say, dad and the board members are getting pretty fed up with me. One more failure and I may find myself soldering integrated circuits in the Texas assembly plant."

He sat back down on her desk, waiting for her response. Frankie blinked at him, dazed. "What—why do you think Grif's behind it?"

"I don't think, I know." Jules was no longer calm. Anger fairly sizzled in his voice. He let his breath out and closed his lips firmly, and Frankie realized he didn't intend to say more.

She shook her head in bewilderment. "I just can't believe it, Jules. Nobody would...what would be the reason?"

"Dad will be retiring in the next few years." The way he spoke of his father made Frankie ache in sympathy. "When he does, it will be in his power to indicate to the board who his successor should be. Grif wants to be president after dad retires. So he makes me look bad to insure that I don't get a crack at it."

He folded his arms and waited while Frankie thought about what he'd said. Grif had fairly reeked of sinister intent. "Just what does Grif do here, anyway?"

"He's vice-president of operations," Jules told her. Again he anticipated her curiosity. "I'm vice-president of research and development. Don't ask if I would have been a VP if my last name weren't Jones." His brief smile held no amusement. "I've never been quite sure myself."

She felt the unwilling stir of compassion his words aroused and suppressed it fiercely. No matter what the circumstances, she knew he wouldn't want her pity. "I don't really give a rat's behind about who's who at Jones Morton," she said bluntly. "The only thing I'm here for is to do the work you hired me to do. I don't intend to politick on the side, or look for an easy permanent berth." She jumped out of her chair and paced impatiently to the window and back. "Jules, I'm starting to get the feeling that this job isn't going to work out. Maybe we'd better agree to tear up my contract—"

Jules's hands came down on her shoulders, forcing her against him. She stared up, wide-eyed, into his face. Through the thin knit of their T-shirts, the heat of their bodies met and made more heat. When he spoke, she could feel the vibrations of his voice.

"You've got to be on my side in this, Frankie." His words were heavy, urgent. "I need success with this electronic security prototype, and I need you to help me get it. You're one of the best systems engineers in the Valley. Everyone you've worked for that personnel contacted said so. You're fast and you're good, and you're here right now. I'm not going to tear up your contract. I'm going to hold you to it."

His grip on her tightened, heightening the electric sensations and making it hard for Frankie to breathe. But Jules seemed oblivious as he stared down at her. Desperately she sucked air into her lungs and had the gratification of seeing his eyes widen and begin to smolder as her breasts moved against his chest. She pushed vainly on his shoulders. "Let me go, damn it!"

He loosened his grip slightly, but it didn't help her much, since his hands shifted to her derriere, pulling her against him with deliberate intent. For a moment she closed her eyes helplessly as hot fire washed through her loins. Jules's husky whisper made her eyes flutter open.

"Frankie?" Yielding to the longing that filled her, she stopped resisting and leaned against him, letting her arms slide around his neck and into the crisp curls of brown hair.

It was sweet to let the overpowering sensations of his kiss flood her. Their lips met and parted, met again in gentle tastes that suddenly fiercely escalated. She was trembling when it ended.

"Jules," she gasped, "how are we going to get any work done? I just don't think this will—"

He laid a finger across her lips. "Hush. People in love have managed to work together before now. We'll manage too."

"People in love?" She twisted out of his grip. "Listen, Jules," she said with determination, "I am not in love with you. You are not in love with me. We experience a ... a strong physical desire for one another, which has been programmed into us by centuries of genetic selection."

He raised an ironic eyebrow. "Indeed. If that's the way you define love, so be it. I happen to be a romantic, but I can accept the scientific view."

"Jules, you're not listening to me!" Frankie was aghast to hear the beginning of a wail in her voice. She walked to the window and took some deep breaths. "Jules," she said when she could trust her voice, "believe me. There is nothing but trouble ahead for us on this project. Let me out of my contract."

"No." There was quiet finality in his voice, and she realized it would be futile to argue further.

"Then can we get to work?"

A reluctant smile crossed his face. "Frankie, you are—" He shook his head helplessly and pulled a chair over beside her desk chair. "Sooner or later," he said, a note of menace in his voice, "we are going to hash out our feelings. But for now, by all means let's work." He pulled the roll of printed circuit layouts toward him and took a pencil out of the desk drawer. "Now, about the power supply."

Frankie stared for a moment, then snapped her mouth shut. "Yes," she said faintly, "there's something I wanted to ask you about that." She sat down beside him in the desk chair, feeling a little limp. Perversely, now that Jules was all business, she had a hard time thinking about the problem at hand. She glanced at the clock with an inward sigh. There were hours to go before she could go home and figure out how she'd gotten herself into such a situation. She focused her concentration on the power supply and settled down to work.

They spent the rest of the day huddled over the drawings, pausing only for a brief break when Jules produced sandwiches at lunchtime. Gradually his declaration of love sank to the back of Frankie's mind. At four o'clock she straightened in her chair, lifted her hair and rubbed the back of her neck. "It won't fly," she announced.

Jules regarded her warily. "It isn't supposed to fly. But I gather you think it won't work."

"Yup." Frankie nodded. "Not the way you have it laid out, anyway." She pointed to one of the drawings. "The layers are far too dense, and the gate arrays are all wrong."

Jules made an impatient movement. "You can fix that, can't you? The overall concept is the important thing here."

"The concept," Frankie said generously, "is brilliant. And yes, I think with a little revision it can be successfully implemented. But these—" She flicked the drawings with one hand and frowned at Jules. "Who did these drawings? It's not very professional work."

"I did them." His voice was smooth, but she could detect an undertone of amusement.

"Oh." Not for anything would she appear flustered.

"I meant what I said this morning, Frankie." Jules leaned toward her, his face intent. Her heart began to pound, but his next words brought her up short. "I made the drawings because I didn't want copies to end up in Grif's hands. You're the only person who's seen them besides me."

She shook her head. "That's not going to increase your chances of success," she told him. "And sooner or later you'll have to give them to the fabrication people so they can make us a prototype board to test." He didn't reply. She looked closely at his rather sheepish expression. "If you're going to ask me to kluge the thing together with vector board and wire wrap, forget it," she added. "I get too much money to fool around with that stuff."

He shook his head stubbornly. "I've got somebody on the outside lined up to make the films and do the board, including stuffing it, so you don't have to worry about soiling your hands with technician work. But no one from inside Jones Morton is going to see it until after the prototype trials. Only you and I will know anything about it until then."

She shrugged, conceding defeat. "You're the boss." The silence stretched between them, and suddenly all the sexual tension was back, sizzling in the air. Frankie moved uneasily to pick up the sheets of drawing paper. "I'll take these home and smooth them up a little," she said, trying somehow to ease the atmosphere. Jules regarded her with a heavy-lidded, knowing gaze. The ancient panic of the hunted creature filled her. "Guess you'd better be going if you want me to get to the calculations." Her words came out breathless.

Jules reached over and put his hand on hers, stilling its feverish scrabbling with the papers. "Work time's over, Frankie," he said huskily. He picked up her hand and brought it to his mouth. His lips nibbled with velvety suggestiveness over the fine bones on the back of her hand. Each contact sent a tiny jolt along her nerve endings. When he turned her hand over and began to nip gently at her palm, she felt her control slipping.

"Jules," she whispered, "the door's open."

He didn't release her hand, but he did lower it from his mouth. "My parents are having a cocktail party tonight," he said abruptly. "I have to go, and I want you to come with me."

Whatever she had expected him to say, it wasn't this. "I—I don't usually go to cocktail parties." She thought of her limited wardrobe. "Why are you asking me?"

The teasing smile was back on his face. "Figure it out for yourself, my Valentine. Pick you up at six-thirty, okay?"

Before she had time to decide he was at the door. "Jules, wait! I was going to go over the drawings tonight."

"The party will be over by eight," he said carelessly. "We can get a pizza or something and go over them together at your place." His expression was smooth and urbane to her suspicious eyes.

"Well," she said grudgingly. "But only if you promise—no playing around. We won't get any work done otherwise."

Jules cast his eyes to the ceiling. "What are you, a workaholic or something?" He took her hand again and dropped a tiny kiss on it. "See you at six-thirty."

JULES'S PARENTS lived high in the foothills west of Palo Alto, in one of the big lavishly decorated showplaces that had begun to crowd out the older, more austere ranch houses and country estates. Their place was a mongrel blend of Spanish mission and California contemporary, with lots of glass walls and hand-painted tiles. The semi-circular driveway was crowded with BMW's, Mercedes and Porsches. Beside them, Jules's Morris Minor had a pleasing air of primness.

Jules steered Frankie through the expensively furnished living room and onto the crowded terrace that edged a swimming pool. There was a bar on one side of the terrace and a buffet table on the other side. Frankie sniffed hungrily. She was used to eating an early dinner.

Jules kept her arm firmly clasped in his as he led her to the bar. Behind it was a taller, older Jules with iron-gray hair receding from the same broad forehead, but a narrow-lipped, sterner mouth. He greeted Jules with a bark of unamused laughter. "About time you showed up, boy. I was beginning to think you wouldn't make it."

Jules ignored this. "Dad, this is Frankie Warburton, the consultant who's helping me with the prototype."

Jeremiah Jones's eyebrows drew together as he studied Frankie; she was engaged in a fearless scrutiny of him. She could see that he'd caught the faint proprietary air in Jules's introduction. After a moment he smiled at her and rumbled out a couple of questions on her impression of Jones Morton. She answered politely, feeling staid and proper in the business suit she was wearing. The only hint of her inner feelings was conveyed by the bright scarlet of her prim silk blouse.

Jules was wrong about his father, she decided. Jeremiah would doubtless be stern as a parent, but there was softness there too. He turned to Jules and shot him a couple of brusque inquiries; Frankie could see the pride in his eyes as Jules gave crisp, informative replies. But a curt nod was all the acknowledgment he allowed his son.

Jules felt the curtness but not the pride. His hands clenched involuntarily as Jeremiah turned back to Frankie. *Dismissed, boy,* he thought cynically. His father had no use for incompetence, but no praise for its opposite. At least the old man could appreciate Frankie. Jules looked at her and forgot his grievances. For a moment, in her proper little suit with her hair wound around her head in a braid, he could view her as a stranger. But only for a moment. Then he remembered the soft tenderness of those beautiful lips, the way her blue eyes were so much more eloquent than her words. When she smiled, he was captivated all over again. Blinking, he brought himself back to the conversation.

"Well, well," his father was saying. "My friend Richard Gillafont mentioned you the other day— spoke very highly of your work on their new personal-development system."

Frankie smiled. "He was easy to work for—let me do most of the design in my home workshop." She sent Jules a teasing look that lodged itself directly into his vitals. Jules closed his eyes for a blissful moment. When he opened them again, his mother was bearing down on them.

Beatrix Jones didn't look too much like the mother of a thirty-five-year-old son. Her body had thickened, her face had sagged a bit, her hair now depended on an exclusive salon for its luster and color. But in other respects she was the same as the girl in the glamorous wedding album she liked to thumb through. Jules mumbled a perfunctory greeting and watched Beatrix deploy his father into the kitchen for more ice. Living should change you, he thought, giving Sheila Madison an absentminded hug as she joined them. It should leave its mark on your face. He looked from his mother to Sheila as they stood together. Sheila was the daughter of his mother's best friend, but their faces were similarly unlined, similar in expression. All the choices, all the traumas—where was the evidence that Beatrix had passed through them? He shook his head.

Frankie's thoughts were running a parallel course. Jules introduced her to his mother, but Beatrix paid little attention to her once she'd uttered the obligatory small talk. Frankie was at leisure to study her as she engaged Jules and Sheila Madison in vivacious conversation. Lovely clothes and a sleek hairstyle weren't enough, Frankie decided. She searched for something of his mother in Jules's face, and was relieved to find very little trace of her there. She had bequeathed to him the full sensuous curve of lip, but his mouth had a firmness that owed more to his own character. Busy with her speculation, Frankie paid little heed to the conversation until Jules touched her arm.

"Okay, Frankie?" His voice was apologetic. "I'll be back in a minute." She watched him walk away with Sheila Madison and caught the other girl's backward complacent glance. *So that's how it's done,* she thought in amused surprise.

Beatrix Jones claimed her attention. "So you're working with my son, Ms Warburton?" The older woman's eyes were sharp at the moment; she no longer bothered with the musical laugh that had punctuated her previous conversation.

Frankie nodded and sipped her wine. She felt an academic, detached interest in what was happening. It was obvious that Beatrix Jones had sensed something between her son and this upstart engineer, and was hastening to contain the damage before it could spread too far. Frankie was prepared for some not-so-subtle probing, but didn't get it; after a few innocuous remarks Jules's mother excused herself with practiced ease.

With the same ease, Beatrix managed to keep Jules away from Frankie for the next hour. He would no sooner finish some little social task than she would have another for him. Frankie didn't mind. She drifted from group to group, occasionally finding someone to talk to, more often just listening and storing up data about a group of people she hadn't had much social intercourse with. Most of the people in attendance were important figures in Silicon Valley—heads of corporations, venture capitalists, the managerial elite. It was interesting to see the lions at feeding time, so to speak. She caught sight of Grif Morton, assiduously plying a prominent banker with drinks and hors d'oeuvres, and slipped behind a screen of giant ferns to avoid being seen by him. She was there when Sheila Madison confronted her.

Sheila was carrying a stemmed, salt-rimmed glass as big as a soup bowl, from which she took a fortifying gulp. "You're one of the engineers at Jones Morton, aren't you?"

Frankie nodded, watching unbelievingly as Sheila

downed another sizable tot of the margarita. "Trix thinks you're gunning for Jules."

It took Frankie a moment to think of a reply to this frontal attack. "Trix? Oh, Jules's mother."

Sheila nodded. She was in her mid-twenties, Frankie decided, with wide ingenuous eyes and a beautiful complexion. Her blond hair swung sleekly around her head. There was an expensive gold bracelet clasped around her slender wrist. "Leave him alone," Sheila said softly.

Frankie raised an eyebrow. She usually avoided scenes, but something told her Sheila would be hard to ignore. "Are you going to tell me why?"

"Because I want him," Sheila said, her childlike voice at variance with the margarita she was rapidly finishing. "If you try to come between us, you'll just get hurt."

Frankie finished her own drink and set the glass down absently in the middle of a dry birdbath. "Does Jules, ah, know you feel like this about him?"

Sheila tossed her shiny hair. "He ought to." Her voice was petulant. "Trix and mother have always intended that we should get married. Jules has just been waiting for me to grow up enough."

Frankie looked at Sheila wonderingly. "When is that going to be do you think?" She was sorry as soon as she'd said the words; catty speeches weren't usually her forte. Sheila seemed so innocuous that it was shameful to make fun of her.

Sheila waved her glass a little wildly and stepped closer. Frankie realized that she must have had several of the big margaritas already. "Listen, working girl, if I want Jules, all I have to do is reach out and take him. I'm just doing you a favor by telling you that it's no use falling for Jules, because he's as good as mine." She ran her contemptuous gaze over Frankie's staid business suit and smoothed her own sleek designer dress. "He doesn't have anything in common with *you*," she added with devastating clarity. "He belongs with me." She took a final swallow of the margarita and threw the big glass at the birdbath. Frankie watched, horrified, expecting a crash. The glass bounced harmlessly into Frankie's. "Only plastic," Sheila said, amusement curling her mouth. "*It* doesn't break." She turned and sauntered back through the ferns.

Frankie was still mulling over the encounter when Jules found her. "What are you doing back here?" He glanced around at the screen of ferns. "On second thought, it's a good idea. I can get away from Trix here."

"You call your mother Trix?" Frankie found that she was a little bothered by the casual disdain in Jules's voice when he spoke of his mother.

"She calls me Jules," he pointed out with inescapable logic. "Are you ready to leave?"

Frankie looked through the ferns at the milling throng on the terrace. The collective sound of the party were starting to get loud, and the buffet table was empty. "Why not?" she said. "The food's all gone."

They drove to her house in near silence. Frankie wanted to ask about Sheila, but couldn't think of any way to frame the question. *Say, Jules, do you and Sheila have some kind of long-standing engagement?* It was better not to bring the subject up.

She felt light-headed from the wine, and from the occasional brush of Jules's arm against hers as he drove. He glanced sideways and caught her looking at him. "What are you thinking about?"

She shook her head, her smile fading. She couldn't

tell him that she was wondering how they could get through the weeks it would take to finish the prototype without succumbing to the passion that sparked so violently between them. And if they did give in, how would it affect their working relationship?

When he spoke it was an uncanny reflection of her own thoughts. "It doesn't have to be an either-or situation, Frankie."

She opened her mouth to ask what he meant, then decided the small evasion wasn't worth the trouble. "Are you reading my mind, Jules?"

"Just your face." He parked the car in front of her house and turned to run his fingers lightly over her cheek and lips. "You have a very expressive face." His lips came down on hers, gently, persuasively. "Don't worry," he whispered against her mouth. "Being lovers won't affect our working relationship."

The touch of his lips against hers was like the turning on of a voltage switch. Frankie felt the power radiating through her body. "We aren't going to be lovers," she whispered back, unable to shut off the current by tearing her mouth away. Instead she found herself acquiescing to the soft seductive touches of his mouth and tongue, closing her eyes and arching against him. When he pulled back an involuntary sound of protest escaped her.

"So we aren't going to be lovers?" His voice was amused. Reluctantly she opened her eyes. "Frankie, how can we avoid it? We want each other, we're in love—"

The words jolted her out of her sensuous trance. "You," she said, pushing him away and reaching for the car door, "say that you're in love with me. Fine and dandy; it's your illusion." She opened the door and turned back to face him defiantly. "I, however, have no romantic little illusions like that. Love is just a word that men and women use to justify their physiological cravings."

She swung her legs out of the car and prepared to march into the house. Jules was on her heels as she unlocked the front door. "Thanks for taking me to the party," she said, turning politely. Her words were spoken into his chest. When she tilted up her head, he grabbed her chin and held her immobile for his scrutiny.

"You really believe that drivel you're putting out." Frankie moved uneasily in his grasp, but he paid no attention to her attempts to free herself. "Frankie, darlin'," he went on gently, "haven't you ever been in love before?"

"I've had...infatuations, based on physical chemistry between the sexes," she replied with stiff dignity. "None of them lasted. Please let me go, Jules."

He released his grip on her chin, transferring it to her arms. "This will last," he said with conviction. "When we've been married twenty years, I'm going to throw your words in your face."

She should have found his calm assumption of marriage funny. Instead it made her angry.

"I have work to do tonight, as I told you before." She shrugged out of his grip and stepped back into her front hall. "If you don't stop talking like a lunatic, I'll—I'll—"

He ignored her efforts to send him away and stepped into the hall with her. "We both have work to do," he said calmly, taking off his jacket uninvited and draping it over a chair as he followed her into the living room. "I'll phone for the pizza while you get the drawings out. What do you like? Pepperoni? Italian sausage?"

"I like to work alone," she snapped. She watched him walk into the kitchen, not wanting to admit that she found something stirring in her heart at the sight of him looking so comfortable in her house. He had done one of his amazing about-faces, switching from the impassioned lover to the brisk engineer faster than Clark Kent switched to Superman. "You have me so confused!"

"I know." He grinned at her before picking up the telephone. "It's part of my technique. Keep 'em guessing. What about anchovies?"

"Ugh," she said automatically. "Listen, Jules, we've got to come to some sort of agreement. No more seduction while I'm working for you."

He paused with the receiver in his hand and looked at her soberly. "I don't like that idea. I don't like it at all."

"Tough." She faced him defiantly. "You don't need all this talk of love and marriage to get me into bed, Jules. I want that as much as you do." She thought she saw his eyes change but it was hard to tell behind the glasses. "But there'll be no action until my job is done at Jones Morton. Those are my conditions for continuing the prototype work. Otherwise I terminate my contract."

His hand tightened on the telephone receiver. Slowly he hung it up. His breath hissed between his teeth. "I am strongly tempted," he said, his voice soft and deadly, "to tear up your contract myself, if that's what it takes to make you admit what we have between us." Her eyes widened a bit at the anger that came through his words.

He walked swiftly over to her and stood, not touching her but so close she could feel his heat. Her legs began to tremble; with an effort she held them still. Now she could see his eyes behind his glasses; they were hard and cold. "However, you are a fine engineer—and you are privy to my design. I prefer that you stay in my sight until that design is implemented." He took a deep breath and turned away. "I accept your conditions, Ms Warburton."

Frankie could not move; she stood staring blankly at the kitchen counter, at the back door and the wall phone beside it, at the edge of the table with its bright yellow-laquered top. She knew by the cool rush of air around her body when Jules opened the front door. A moment later came the soft thud of the door shutting. Something wet fell on her tightly clenched hands. With numb surprise she realized it was a tear.

4

THE BALL ARCED through the high, limitless expanse of sky toward Frankie's waiting baseball glove. It fell with an illusion of immobility, seeming not to fall but to grow larger with astonishing speed. She raised her glove, her body arching into the air in its turn as the ball smacked into the deep leather pocket. A jubilant grin lit her face; she cradled the ball briefly, then hurled it toward the second base man.

Jules waited to see the double play completed before he turned away, glad for the dark glasses that would hide his expression from any interested spectator. He swung a bat idly to warm up for his turn at the plate, but his thoughts weren't on the softball game. His thoughts, as usual this past week, were on Valentine Frances Warburton.

It had been excruciating to put in ten-hour days working closely with her, wanting her, loving her and not being able to say it. Out in the sun, feeling isolated among the partying throng at the department picnic, he could admit that he had been interpreting her demand to curtail the lovemaking in a rather sadistic spirit. He had been cold, scrupulously polite, unbendingly distant, hoping all the time that it would move her, force her out of her untenable position, make her explode somehow with the passion he knew was in her.

Instead, she had retreated further each day, only

occasionally showing the hurt in her eyes that stabbed him with an unconscious rebuke. All week he had justified his behavior on the grounds that he had no lukewarm emotions where Frankie was concerned. If he was not allowed to express his love, his need, he could not pretend that only friendly feelings existed between them. He exhaled impatiently. Why did he have to fall for a woman who was so closed up to love? Even now, at the departmental softball game, they were on different sides.

The umpire called third out before it was his turn to bat. Jogging to his position in right field, he passed Frankie coming in. She was flushed with the sun and exercise. The short, fine hairs around her face had escaped from the clip at the nape of her neck. She had on a T-shirt with California poppies on it, and cut-off blue jeans. He felt his body go tight at the emotion that flooded him. She was so beautiful.

"Hi, Jules." Her smile was uncertain. He was filled with remorse for his treatment of her. She paused in front of him, and vaguely he realized that he had taken her hand and pulled her to a stop.

"Frankie," he said, fighting the incoherent words that rose to his lips. She waited, her smile growing broader as he hesitated. "Listen, let's eat together. I—I want to show you something."

It was her turn to hesitate. "Is that a good idea? I mean...."

His hand moved involuntarily to smooth the hair away from her face. She went very still at the touch of his fingers. "Please. I'll behave."

"Well, all right." She jerked away from his hand, looking around in nervous confusion. "They want to clear the field. I have to go."

He found his place in right field and stood there, a blissful smile on his face, while the center fielder ran for all the hits. Surely, today she would see— she had to see.

FRANKIE PERCHED IN THE BLEACHERS to wait for her turn at bat. She should have been cheering for her teammates, but instead she watched Jules miss a couple of easy ones, turning on that goofy grin when the center fielder shouted at him to wake up. All week he'd been like a robot, coldly efficient, totally in control of his emotions. It had shaken her up; she had worked long hard hours just to finish her contract quickly and get out of a situation that confused and hurt her so much. If only she hadn't issued that smart-alecky warning of hers—if only Jules hadn't taken it so seriously! But his icy behavior had made it impossible for her to reopen the subject, and so she had retreated behind her own wall of indifferent courtesy. She watched Jules botch a line drive and laughed out loud. Life was looking better.

"It's no laughing matter, young lady." The severe voice beside her was half familiar. She turned with the smile still lingering on her lips.

"Oh hello, Mr. Jones." Jules's father eased himself onto the splintery wooden bench beside her, looking natty and comfortable in a knit polo shirt and white duck trousers. "I didn't realize you were at the picnic."

He waved a hand. "Just taking a look in, that's all." He scowled at the field, where Jules stood gazing abstractedly into the middle distance instead of crouching for instant readiness. "The boy usually plays better than that. Don't know what he's thinking about."

Frankie didn't reply, though she felt her lips curving in a slight secret smile.

"Lacks the competitive instinct." Jeremiah Jones shook his head. "He'll never be a success without it." He looked at his laced fingers with much the same expression as Jules wore. "Grif, now—he's different."

"Everybody's different, or should be," Frankie pointed out. Jeremiah started as if the bleachers had spoken.

"Ah, Miss Warburton. Naturally you feel I'm slighting the engineering aspects when I deplore Jules's attitude. But if there's one thing I've learned over the last twenty years it's that the best product in the world goes nowhere if you don't know how to sell it."

Frankie shook her head stubbornly. "The best salesman in the world makes nothing if he's got nothing worth selling too. Jules has a very fine, creative intelligence. He's one of the people who come up with the kind of technological breakthroughs that keep us all in business."

The old man wasn't displeased by this frank speech. "He's a good boy," he said gruffly. "But he will fritter his time away with painting and poetry and all that nonsense. He needs to learn to focus his energy, like Grif does."

Frankie opened her mouth to argue, remembering the way Jules had focused himself on work during the last week. But this wasn't her business, after all. "I'd better go warm up to bat," she said instead.

Jeremiah Jones surprised her by taking her hand for a moment. "Thanks for giving me a bit of back talk, young lady." His gaze strayed out to the playing field and softened. "It's not a topic I'm very objective about." He pinned her again with that knowing stare, so like Jules's expression. "And maybe you're not objective either," he said, chuckling. "Get along with you, now."

The game was over by twelve-thirty, Frankie's team winning. Jules pulled her away from her gleeful teammates who swarmed around the big cooler that held the beer.

"C'mon," he said in an urgent undertone that had her moving briskly without quite realizing it. They were in his Morris and chugging away before she spoke.

"I thought we were going to eat lunch."

He kept his eyes on the road. "We are."

She looked back toward the picnic site. Several of the long tables were dotted with a tempting array of potluck dishes. A large charcoal grill to one side held thick slabs of aromatic meat. "Jules," she said gently, "we're driving away from the food." His lips quirked, but he didn't reply. "Jules, I'm hungry. *Really* hungry." He was still silent. "You know, people who play hard and win softball games get sort of starved, sort of faint...."

"Don't worry," he said at last, his voice silky with promise. "You won't faint." He glanced at her, just for a second. The blaze of his eyes made her catch her breath. "I plan to feed you too," he added.

She swallowed, feeling a fire of anticipation race through her. "Where—where are we going?"

"My place." There was no mistaking the sensuality that laced his voice. "Thought you might like to see it."

They drove in silence for a while, winding down out of the hills that cradled the park. The narrow roads were exhilarating in the bright May sunlight.

Below them, Stanford's Hoover Tower seemed to hold up the blue arch of the sky. Past the thickly clustered cities of the peninsula, San Francisco Bay sparkled like lapis lazuli. Beyond it the green-brown hills of the East Bay stretched into the distance.

Jules pulled over for a moment and put the top down on the Morris, letting the cool fragrant air rush over them. When they reached the flatland she sighed regretfully.

They worked their way north on Highway 280, then turned east toward the bay on a succession of roads. Frankie grew curious. "Where do you live, anyway?" Her voice broke the silence.

"Where did you think I'd live?" He flicked an intent glance at her, turning off on a road that led to the port of Redwood City. She shrugged helplessly.

"In a condo—in a house in the hills—I don't know."

He lived on a houseboat, anchored near a small harbor complex in Redwood City. She was entranced with the tidy little boat. It was moored at the far end of one of the docks, next to the low dusty green swell of marshland that edged the channel leading out into San Francisco Bay. She laughed as she took in the name on the square transom.

"The *Nautilus*? Wasn't that Captain Nemo's boat?" The moody, half-crazed captain of Jules Verne's *Twenty-Thousand Leagues Under the Sea* had been one of her favorite characters since she'd read the book at age eleven.

Jules helped her down into the low cabin. It was charming, with a tiny kitchen at the far end of the room. To her right a triangular desk had been built into the corner beside the door.

Before her were two steps down, leading to the living area. It was small—about eight feet square—surrounded with low cabinets built into the walls and gleaming with brass. Colorful cushions in front of and on top of the cabinets provided places to perch. In each side wall were double portholes, also with gleaming brass work. Under the one on the right, a Japanese futon had been placed to make a wide couch. It would fold out, Frankie knew, to create a bed almost as large as the living space. Perhaps for that reason, aside from the futon and cushions, there were no other furnishings.

Jules kicked his shoes off and stepped down into the living area, opening one cabinet. Behind its shiny mahogany face there was a first-class stereo system. He put on soft, jazzy music and turned to face Frankie.

"Japanese style," he said, his hand sweeping around the houseboat's interior. "The only way to live in a small space." His smile glinted. "Not much like Captain Nemo."

She walked past the built-in desk, past another door that must be the bathroom, past a louvered closet, toward the carpeted steps that led down into the living area. The surroundings seemed to her at once austere and sensuous, with the soft carpets and futon, the hard gleam of brass and wood fittings. The furnishings were spare and uncomplicated, but luxurious all the same.

She sank down on the floor and leaned against a couple of immense pillows. "I'll admit Captain Nemo didn't seem to spend much time lolling about in his *Nautilus*." Frankie wriggled a little farther into the pillows and nodded. "Definitely lolling."

He stood by the porthole, watching her. When

their eyes met the air in the little room seemed to thicken, making it difficult to breathe. Jules's look showed stark hunger, undisguised need. Frankie's body began to ache with desire.

He came toward her, pulling his sweat-soaked T-shirt off and tossed it into the closet. She stared at the smoothly muscled, tanned torso and felt the tension inside her become almost unbearable. He knelt beside her and with a hand that shook slightly, he reached for the clip that held her hair. The long silky strands slid through his fingers. His hands burrowed under the curtain of hair to find her shoulders, pulling her to him.

She felt her bones turn to honey as his warm palms slipped down her back and up again in a slow massage. Jules's eyes were very bright, burning with a heart-stopping message. "Frankie," he breathed, running the heels of his hands along her sides, almost brushing the quivering fullness of her breasts. "Darlin', I'm famished. I want a kiss. Just one kiss, please, love...."

Logical thought was impossible when her nerve endings were reacting so wildly. She gave up on trying to analyze every action and gave in to her desire to assuage his hunger. "Oh, Jules, of course—" His lips were on hers, swallowing the rest of her incoherent utterance, touching her lips so softly it was almost painful, bringing her blood to an instant high boil. Her body cried out for more, but his mouth was retreating, touching, teasing...she felt a frustrated moan escape her. The next time his lips touched, she flicked her tongue out in delicate, deliberate provocation.

The response was immediate. He crushed her to him, surging into her mouth like hot sweet fire, thrusting their bodies together so she could feel his imperative need. She met the kiss eagerly, her body curling against his, knowing that she wanted it to happen between them, that she couldn't deny this feeling.

His thumbs rode lightly over her swollen nipples. She arched upward, trying to capture his hand for her aching fullness. Her eyelids passion heavy, she watched the heady wonder on his face as his hands moved slowly over her breasts. She made an unconscious noise in her throat and he snatched her against him again, his face buried in her hair.

Jules tried to get control of his ragged breathing. This wasn't exactly the way he'd meant for things to go. He'd intended to bring her here, give her a lighthearted lunch in the sunshine, make a gentle pass or two and then take her home, demonstrating his self-control, keeping things slow so as not to scare her off again. But as soon as she walked in his door he'd been all over her. He took another deep breath and lifted his head to look at her. She met his eyes candidly. They both spoke at once.

"Jules, I'm sorry—"

"Frankie, I'm sorry—"

"You first," Jules decided generously. Frankie gave him a saucy smile.

"I'm not about to apologize if you're going to. Let's hear it, Captain Nemo."

Jules grinned and picked up one of her hands, nibbling at each finger in succession. "You know, I always thought Captain Nemo was a pretty passionate kind of guy," he said between nibbles. "I bet if he hadn't been a Victorian he could have seduced the pants off some of those women."

His tongue circled her palm, and Frankie found herself oddly breathless. "This is not an apology, but I guess I won't press my luck," she said, striving to keep her voice even. "After all, I didn't exactly fight you off."

Jules searched her face and smiled with relief. "I really will feed you." He got to his feet, his smile reflecting sensual promise. "Anything you want."

Frankie swallowed. She wanted more of the appetizer. She could live forever on that.

Jules pulled deli containers out of the refrigerator and piled them on a tray, along with a bottle of wine and two lovely crystal wineglasses. They sat cross-legged on the soft carpeting, the tray between them. They fed each other crackers spread with pâté and soft ripe cheese. Scorning forks, they ate marinated mushrooms and big fat olives with their fingers, which they licked with abandon. The wine was dark and a little savage, a Barbera bottled by one of Jules's friends. They drank most of the bottle before the meal was finished.

Frankie nibbled the last olive from Jules's fingers, then stretched voluptuously, letting the warmth of the wine stir the embers of her simmering sexual tension. She didn't want the afternoon to end without Jules in her arms. But judging from the restraint he'd shown earlier, he still remembered her hasty speech of the previous week. If she wanted him today, she would have to show him that it was all right.

He sat the depleted tray on a counter in the tiny kitchen and turned to look at her. As their eyes met she felt herself begin to melt. She had never seen that expression on a man's face directed at her—the burning need, the desire and something else, something that made her heart pound.

She cleared her throat, searching for something innocuous to say. "So...great game this morning."

His eyes crinkled intriguingly behind his glasses.

"Only the winner could think so. From my point of view, it was a disaster."

There was another moment of heavy silence between them. Frankie tore her gaze away from Jules, and noticed that the walls around the cabin above the dark mahogany of the cupboards were hung with a few watercolors and pencil sketches. She jumped to her feet to examine them. Between one set of portholes a round trompe l'oeil porthole had been painted, opening onto an underwater scene that depicted various kinds of fish relaxing in some surprising ways.

"I didn't know octopuses went in for physical fitness." In the background of the picture an octopus, running shoes on each of its eight legs, jogged placidly along the ocean floor. "Or is it octopi?"

He joined her, draping a casual arm around her shoulder. "I especially had fun with the fishy fish." In one corner of the scene, some unsavory looking tuna were evidently trading threats.

Frankie moved a little closer to him, increasing the amount of body contact and sending her own sensors on red alert. She hoped the same thing was happening to Jules. "I—what are those fish doing?" He didn't answer for a moment and she moved again, the point of her breast nudging his side. "Those ones there. The carp."

His arm tightened on her shoulder, his hand slipping up and down her arm in a slow caress. "It should be obvious what they're doing," he growled softly.

The carp were certainly tangled in a passionate embrace, unhindered by their superfluity of fins. "I didn't think that fish...made love like that." Her voice came out husky: The touch of Jules's fingers on her arm, the feel of his warm breath on her cheek, scented with the sharp tang of wine—all combined to make her giddy with desire.

Jules turned her to face him. He took off his glasses and put them aside, his eyes blazing with emotion. Frankie could see all she wanted to see in that branding look—all and more. Its brightness was so fierce she could scarcely bear it.

Time seemed to slow, perhaps because her heart was beating so fast. The patch of sunlight they stood in was as golden as honey. It poured over Frankie as she pulled off her T-shirt and wrapped her arms around Jules's bare bronze chest. She felt the sensations in each individual nerve ending. The tips of her breasts, throbbing with hunger, touched the crisp curling hair, and the skin beneath.

Jules's eyes darkened, then drifted shut in delight as the small, hard peaks of her breasts pushed into him. Frankie stared in wonder at the pleasure and strain on his face, feeling the way he trembled. Reaching up, she pulled his face down to hers. "I want you to make love to me, Jules," she whispered against his lips. "Right now, that's all I want."

His hands slid around to her back to hold her closely, tenderly. "Oh, Frankie. Oh, sweetheart, if you're sure—"

She kissed him, hoping that the fire that seared her own lips was burning him, telling him what she could not put into words. She let her hands wander over the sleek muscles of his back, getting pleasure shocks from the feel of his skin.

"Frankie, love," Jules breathed, sliding his hands along her shoulders, down her arms, bringing them at last to touch the satiny skin that pressed against his chest. He loved the way she played the wanton with such underlying innocence. He loved

the sweet animal noises she made as he slipped off
the rest of their clothing. He knelt to unfold the
futon, then turned away, opening a cupboard con-
taining a row of drawers. He began to hunt blindly
through one of the drawers. Frankie guessed what
he searched for.

"I—I took care of that," she whispered. He looked
back at her, questioning. "In the bathroom...before
lunch." A blush rose from her chest to spread rosy
color over her face. He smiled lovingly and pulled
her gently to her knees, facing him on the soft surface of the mat.

They kissed, their mouths barely touching, letting the heat build to intolerable levels before
breaking off for air. Jules buried his face in the
hollow of her neck, his mouth still avid on her
skin. He burned fire down the slope of her chest,
and her head fell back to encourage him. When
his lips and tongue took gentle possession of one
nipple, Frankie felt the heat explode within her.
She clenched his lean buttocks with her hands and
arched fiercely against his body. Her tongue flicked
out to taste the skin of his shoulder, still faintly
salty from the exertions of the ball game. There
was nothing scented or store-bought about his
smell—it was a compound of sweat and something
stronger, something primordially male. She took a
deep breath of it and rubbed her body tantalizingly
against his.

He shuddered and let his hands roam down the
length of her until they searched out her heart of
fire, bringing her to the blazing point. She reached
blindly to hold him, to goad him, and he gasped
into her ear, "That's right, love, touch me, oh, so
good...." Finally he laid her gently back against
the cushions and stilled her insistent body with

slow aching entry, each movement accompanied
by their amazed amorous cries, their bodies demanding, receiving, teasing, building. She could
not look away from his eyes, from their inflaming
expression, until at last the fires were too consum-
ing and she had to close her own eyes and let the
fierce storm rush through her.

THEY LAY SPRAWLED on the futon in a tangle of damp
arms and legs, Frankie's hair tumbling wildly over
the cushions. She sighed and opened her eyes,
smiling blissfully into Jules's bemused face.

"Is that how it always is?" Her whisper held
wonder. She reached up to trace the line of his jaw
tenderly. "Because if so, I really have been missing
out."

His smile broadened. "That's how it is when you
love someone," he told her. "It's the love that
makes it so."

She twisted uneasily. "Jules," she began, "I
thought—"

"All right, all right, I'll spare you the lecture on
how you can tell love from lust."

"I'd rather experiment about it anyway," she
said, trailing her fingers down his neck and along
his chest. "How does this feel to you?" She circled
his nipple with her finger, watching him with interest. "Is it exciting? Huh? I mean, it gets *me* going, so I just wondered if it's the same for you."

He gulped. "Well, it's...."

"Here, let me try this." She moved to kiss his
chest, letting her teeth take tiny stinging nips of the
smooth flesh. His rib cage rose as he took a deep
breath, and she leaned back to smile innocently
into his face. The expression she saw there sent a
fresh tremor of excitement coursing through her.

Jules could take no more teasing. He moved swiftly to pin Frankie back against the bed, his body hard and ready against the juncture of her thighs. "My turn," he growled, his hands caressing the softness of her breasts, his fingers plucking the nipples till they stood at attention. When he drew each proud crest in turn into his mouth, sucking and nipping in gentle homage, she began to writhe beneath him, wrapping her legs around him, demanding fulfillment. He rolled over and leaned back against the cushions, pulling her slowly and erotically on top of him.

When their bodies joined they were still for a moment, their hands entwined, their eyes locked together, exchanging a silent message. *I love you, Frankie,* Jules's eyes said, although he wasn't aware of it. But in her eyes, he saw something flicker and grow strong. *I love you, Jules.* He closed his eyes thankfully and clasped her to him, losing himself in the wild thrusts of their lovemaking. Now the only difficulty was to get her to realize she loved him and say it out loud.

5

THE PHONE RANG, rousing Frankie from a contentment that amounted almost to stupor. She stretched as Jules padded across the carpet to answer it. The phone was near a window that aureoled his body with light, and she let her eyes roam lazily over his strong sinewy limbs. When she reached his face in her survey, she found him smiling at her.

He listened for a moment after saying hello, an expression of fond resignation on his face. "My team lost, dad," he said. Not wishing to overhear his conversation, Frankie gathered up her clothes and moved toward the tiny bathroom off the kitchen. Her body felt different—soft and a little tremulous, a little tentative. The boat's small cabin seemed full of low, slanting sunbeams and water reflections; it was redolent with the musky scent of their lovemaking.

The bathroom was crowded with a basin, a toilet and a very skinny shower stall that lured Frankie irresistably. She turned the taps on, a bit taken aback by the low water pressure. In the close confines of the bathroom, the scent of lovemaking was not nearly so transcendental. "I need a shower," she muttered, and stepped into the stall.

Jules found her trying to scrub her back and hold her hair out of the way at the same time. "Need a little help, lady?"

"This shower isn't big enough for both of us."

She stuck out her tongue at his suggestive look. "Too bad. We can take a shower at my place someday."

"Showers are all right if you just want to get clean," he told her, taking the washcloth away and plying it briskly up and down her back. "For what you're thinking about, we need the hot tub."

"Why do you think I'm thinking about what you're obviously thinking about?" She directed her gaze pointedly down his torso. "Wait a minute—are you saying you have a hot tub on this boat?" Surprised, she let her hair fall into the spray of the shower. Sodden strands plastered themselves over her shoulders. "Rats. I guess I might as well wash it."

Jules handed her a bottle of shampoo. "The hot tub's on the rear deck." He pointed vaguely in that direction. "There's some boat traffic but if you want to skinny-dip, I'm game." He smiled teasingly.

"I'll wait." She stole a look at him from under the mass of shampoo. "Unless you happen to have a few left over ladies' swimsuits lying around." She thought of Sheila Madison. When Jules shook his head to her subtle prying, she felt a primitive rush of relief that surprised her in its intensity. She didn't like the implications. There was no place for jealousy in logical thought. She groped for a change of topic.

"Bet your father was upset with you for losing the ball game."

"I didn't lose it single-handedly," Jules pointed out mildly.

"He seemed to think you were this morning. He watched from the bleachers with me for a minute, and implied that you usually play better than you did today."

Jules stepped into the tiny shower, crowding Frankie up to the wall. "Come off it," he said huskily in her ear, his hands smoothing the water from her body with tingling strokes. "You know what was wrong with me this morning. How can anyone expect me to play ball when I only want to play with Frankie—"

Laughing, Frankie pushed his hands away. "You're all sweaty, and I was all clean," she protested.

Jules rubbed his body against hers, the water letting her breasts slide with a tantalizing trace of friction across the rough terrain of his chest. Frankie felt a fresh surge of desire that made her lean against the back of the shower. "No fair," he said hoarsely, pulling her upright again. "I scrubbed your back, now you have to scrub mine." He handed her the washcloth and turned his back to her.

Frankie took the cloth and swished it over his back, liking the feel of smooth supple muscle, noticing that his skin was lightly freckled. He gave a telltale flinch when she rubbed the cloth over his side, and she pounced gleefully on the hint.

"Oh, are you ticklish? Surely not!" She poked him gently in the ribs and was rewarded with a definite squirm. "Gracious sakes, will you look at that!" She ran her fingers lightly along his ribs and the vulnerable flesh just above his waist. He dissolved into helpless, writhing laughter. "This big, strong, macho engineer is rendered helpless by a little tickling! He—"

Jules began to retaliate. He found the sensitive spots on her neck and used them without mercy. "Witch, you won't...get off lightly...." She tried to regain her advantage but he held her against the back of the shower until she was giggling hysterically. "Now you see," he hissed in melodramatic tones, "what happens to those who oppose Captain Nemo!" His hands slid suggestively along her body, making her wriggle, but not from being tickled. "For you, the punishment will fit the crime. You are doomed never to leave this boat, never to find your clothes again."

"But Captain!" Frankie squeaked. "I'm innocent!"

"Not any more you're not." Abruptly Jules abandoned the game. Holding her to him, he turned so the water ran down her back, rinsing the remaining shampoo from her hair. "Gotta get going, love." When her hair was free of bubbles he ran his hands down her body one last time, ostensibly to remove the last traces of soap, then turned off the water. He pulled her out and wrapped them both in a bath towel almost as big as the room, with another towel for her hair. "Dad wants us to come over for dinner tonight." His voice was light, but Frankie detected a grim undertone that made her scrutinize his face. "Do you—would you like to go?"

Again memories of that uncomfortable cocktail party floated through her mind. "Well," she said slowly, "is this a—a party, or a family thing, or what?"

He watched her, his eyes intent, his face unsmiling. "I didn't ask. But dad's taken a fancy to you, and when he heard you were with me, he asked us over." His laugh was mirthless. "I doubt he would have asked me if I'd been alone, so you can take that as a compliment."

In her secret thoughts about what might happen this evening, Frankie had envisioned them sharing takeout food in her cozy kitchen, or dining at a table for two in an intimate restaurant. But Jules's tone made her curious about the relationship between himself and his parents. "All right," she said agreeably. "Let's go there. Hope your mother realizes that my softball-playing clothes are actually the latest in designer sportswear. I understand everyone's wearing them to dinner parties on the east coast."

"I thought we'd just wear the towel and go as Roman Siamese twins." Jules fitted her against his side and draped the towel in a tasteful toga that barely covered Frankie's breasts. They went sideways through the narrow door, trying to match their steps.

"This isn't working," Frankie gasped, weak with laughter. "I don't believe being joined with the towel is adequate to approximate Siamese twins."

Jules tumbled them both to the rumpled surface of the futon. She caught her breath at the blaze in his eyes. "I know how we should be joined," he whispered, unwrapping the towel.

Frankie swallowed and shut her eyes, feeling the heat rise in her body. "Is this in the nature of an experiment, Dr. Jones?" She wound her arms around him, arching against him. "Because if so, I'd like to participate."

His lips began a leisurely journey along her collarbone and down her breast. "Believe me, Dr. Warburton," he breathed between gentle nips and kisses, "your very active participation is strongly encouraged."

Neither of them wanted the afternoon to end; they prolonged it as long as possible. Before they left the boat Jules insisted on helping her comb her hair. He knelt behind her on the futon, parting the tangles with patient fingers, using the comb far more gently than Frankie did. "Is your hair a lot of trouble? I love it long, but I figured long hair must take too much time or all women would have it."

Frankie shrugged, enjoying the feel of his hands in her hair. She closed her eyes and let her head sink forward on her knees. "It isn't that bad, really. Combing it after shampooing is the worst, but after that I just tie it back. The trouble with short hair is that you have to keep getting haircuts. *That's* a royal hassle—putting yourself in the hands of some weirdo who remembers that you didn't tip him well enough last time."

He pulled her to her feet. "C'mon, let's go. I think I like playing ladies' maid, but the part I'm waiting for is when you start getting dressed for the party."

JULES'S IDEA OF HELPING was to go through her closet, saying nothing about its sparse contents, but pouncing on the black silk jump suit in its cleaner's bag. "Aha!" He laid it on the bed and started toward Frankie. "If ma'amselle would allow me to disrobe her," he said in a thick, bogus French accent, "we could soon accomplish the dressing."

"Sounds like you're stuffing a turkey," Frankie protested. "Are you sure that's what I should wear?" She glanced doubtfully at the jump suit, remembering its revealing lines.

"It reminds me of our first date." Jules stripped the cleaner's bag away. "Which drawer has the sexy little panties in it?"

"No drawer. I mean, I don't have any," Frankie said, steering him firmly toward the door. "If you don't mind, I think I'll do better myself."

"Please don't throw me out. I'll be good." He adopted an attitude of mock humility. "I'll just sit on the bed and keep my mouth shut. You won't even know I'm here."

He was as good as his word, but Frankie was acutely aware of his presence as she got out her plain and practical underclothes. She had been gloriously unselfconscious about her body throughout the afternoon on his boat, but undressing in front of him in her bedroom gave her a sudden attack of the jitters. She picked up the jump suit and glanced at him sideways. "I—I think I'll get dressed in Sarabeth's room, if you don't mind," she said, suddenly whisking out of the door and down the hall before he could answer. She went into Sarabeth's bedroom and shut the door, feeling absurdly relieved. Quickly she pulled on her clothes. "Stupid to make such a song and dance,"she scolded herself under her breath. Sarabeth's bureau was crowded with pots and bottles. Frankie put on some mascara and experimented with blusher, deciding she liked her face rosy. She picked up a pair of ebony combs and pulled her hair back from her face with them. Too bad Sarabeth was away for the weekend and couldn't enjoy the transformation of her roommate from practical engineer to novice vamp.

She went back to her room for her shoes. Jules was stretched out on her bed, his eyes closed, his chest rising and falling rhythmically. She felt a wave of tenderness pass over her. He looked good on her bed. He looked like part of her life. She pushed that thought away hastily and cleared her throat.

"Jules? Shouldn't we get going?" He didn't wake up and she stepped closer, reaching out a hand to rouse him. He moved then, pulling her on top of his sprawled figure. "You weren't asleep!"

"I was playing possum," he admitted shamelessly. His eyes opened. "You look like an angel," he murmured. Her hair cascaded around her shoulders, forming a golden curtain. He ran his hands through it. "Why are we dallying here, woman? We've got to go."

They took his Morris, talking comfortably on the drive to the hills. Their conversation took in the prototype project, then wandered to gardening, books, music. When they turned into the steep winding drive that led to the Jones's hilltop home, Frankie found herself once again curious about the evening before her.

"Will there be lots of people there tonight or is it just family?"

Jules shrugged. "It's never just family on Saturday night, but I didn't ask who else Trix snagged for dinner."

Once again Frankie felt an odd shock at hearing Jules mention his mother. "Do you call your father Jeremiah, or Jerry, or whatever?" She kept her voice carefully neutral, aware that she was probing into an emotional issue, but unable to keep from asking.

Jules slanted her an amused look as he parked the Morris in the circular drive. "Dad doesn't mind being a father, although he does mind a bit that he's mine instead of Grif's. He never invited me to call him anything but dad. However, Trix would really prefer not to be called mom." He turned and took Frankie's face between his hands, trapping her gaze with his own. "It's sweet of you to worry about my feelings," he told her, accurately interpreting the faint distress in her eyes. "But I long ago gave up wishing for the TV-family kind of closeness in my family that you seem to think I pine for. My dad and I disagree, but we have strong ties for all of that. And Trix—'' He shrugged. ''We each have lives we like, and we don't get in each other's way.'' He moved his hands to Frankie's shoulders and gave her a gentle squeeze. ''Now let's go in, have dinner, be civilized and get away as early as possible. Okay?''

Frankie nodded and smiled, but Jules's words had done nothing to dismiss her uneasiness. His voice was too brittle, his words too flip, when he spoke of his parents. She sensed that there was more than met the eye.

The house was lit extravagantly in the early dusk, with spotlights pointing out some architectural coup, or some landscaping triumph. Inside, the lights were dimmer, the smells of furniture polish and flowers mingling with an underlying musky scent. A babble of voices came from the archway to the left. Jules led Frankie through the door, pausing for an instant to look around. Frankie swept the room full of people with a glance and her heart sank.

There weren't actually that many guests. She looked around again as Jules took her over to his father, who was talking to a man about his own age, gesturing with animation. Jeremiah Jones caught sight of Frankie and Jules and broke off his conversation, his smile growing broader.

''Well, look who's here. Congratulations on winning the game, Ms Frances Warburton.''

Frankie put her hand into his and grinned. ''It was close, Mr. Jones. And everyone played well.''

''Everyone except this butterfingers here.'' Jeremiah Jones gave his son a fierce scowl. *Why, the old man dotes on him,* Frankie realized. It might not be obvious to Jules, but Jeremiah's gruff manner was probably a defense against the strong emotions he felt for his son. Her revelation was so blinding that it took her a moment to bring her attention back to the conversation. When she did, Jules's father was telling her to call him Jeremiah. "No sense in this 'Mr. Jones' stuff," he said, clapping the man who stood with him on the back. "I'm Jeremiah, and this is Stan Morton. Stan and I have been teamed up since the days of vacuum tubes, although he doesn't want to be involved in the business end of things anymore."

The other man smiled vaguely and shook Frankie's hand with a surprisingly strong grip. "The good old days," he said to Jeremiah. "I find the theoretical work that Jules does fascinating, but I simply cannot be interested in the applications." He turned to Frankie. "Are you working for Jones Morton, Miss—er, Frances?"

"You must call me Frankie," she said firmly. "And yes, I'm currently doing some contract work for Jules."

"Frankie's too modest," Jules put in, giving Stan an affectionate smile. "She's one of the best microprocessor designers in the Valley. I was lucky to get her." Frankie squirmed a little in the firm grip of his arm. Smoothly he turned the conversation. "How are the orchids doing?"

Stan Morton's face lit up. "Wonderfully. I got the new greenhouse up day before yesterday. What a job! I think all the pieces were mislabeled. I've had several requests for my new hybrid, you know, and now I have room to propagate."

Frankie was immediately interested. "Do you grow orchids? I've always wanted to try them, but they simply don't like my house. They always die."

Stan Morton moved closer to her. "Really? Which direction does your house face?"

A faint waft of scent heralded the arrival of Jules's mother, and Stan's question was left unanswered. Beatrix Jones stood by Jeremiah's arm, smiling prettily and waiting for silence. When she had it she spoke in a soft voice that nevertheless could be heard by everyone in the room.

"How nice to see you again, Miss Warrenton. Jules, darling, could I ask you to help me for a moment?"

"Sorry, Trix," Jules said easily, tightening his grip on Frankie. "I had too much psychic damage in the ball game to be of help to anyone. Why don't you ask Grif?" He nodded toward the other side of the room, where Grif Morton was just turning away from the bar with a fresh drink. Catching Grif's eye, Jules smiled affably. Grif started toward them.

"Really, dear," Trix began, her voice less resonant. "I couldn't ask Grif to do this—"

"Sure you could," Jules said as Grif halted by Jeremiah Jones. "Trix needs some social assistance of some kind, buddy. You up for it?"

Grif smiled politely. "Naturally, Trix. What can I do?" His eyes drifted over the crowd and stopped with an expression that, in anyone else, Frankie would have called warmth. "Perhaps you'd like me to take Jules's place with Miss Madison?"

There was a jarring note in Grif's voice that Jules didn't seem to notice. But Frankie did, and she could see that it hadn't escaped Trix either. Her hostess's face suddenly became thoughtful, and she allowed herself to be led away. "It's kind of you, dear boy," they heard her say.

"Now, Stan—" Jules began, then bit off his words. He looked across the room where Grif was greeting the beautiful and sulky young woman who had accosted Frankie at the cocktail party. His eyes widened. "Gamma!" His exclamation was an exuberant shout.

"Yes, I meant to tell you on the phone, Jules. That's what I called for really." But Jeremiah's words were spoken to Jules's back. Jules was striding across the room, straight toward Sheila Madison. Frankie stood, bereft, bewildered. The undercurrents of relationships and expectations that swirled beneath the party atmosphere were beginning to oppress her. A triumphant smile began to dawn on Sheila Madison's face, with a corresponding glower from Grif. Both expressions turned to bewilderment when Jules pushed past them toward the archway leading out of the large room. A small, spry-looking white-haired woman stood there, a broad smile showing the deep creases in her face as she looked up at Jules. He hugged her with gentle ferocity and began to lead her toward Frankie.

"Mother lives in Monterey, but she arrived for a visit this afternoon quite unexpectedly." Jeremiah Jones beamed fondly at his mother as Jules escorted her across the floor.

Jules brought his grandmother up and introduced her to Frankie. "Gamma, this is my special lady, Miss Valentine Frances Warburton. Frankie, my all-time favorite woman, Mrs. Elizabeth Jones."

Frankie gravely shook hands with Mrs. Jones, who assessed her with one shrewd glance. "You're nice looking in the best way, my dear." Her voice sounded old, but strong, with the penetrating quality of someone beginning to experience hearing loss. "Not like a lot of the modern girls." Without waiting for Frankie's response, she turned to her son. "I'm glad to see you're inviting a few real people, Jeremiah. Get some life into this mausoleum." She looked disparagingly around the elegant room. "Trix never opens any windows. If she dressed more warmly she wouldn't be afraid of a little breeze now and then."

"Did you mention my name, mother?" Trix drifted up to her husband's arm and turned on her sweet smile.

"Yes, I did, Beatrix. If you'd just put on a few more clothes, you could have the windows open once in a while." Jules had put an arm around Frankie's shoulders again, and she felt him shake with suppressed laughter. "When you begin to get old," the old lady told her daughter-in-law kindly, "you need to conserve the body heat. I'll give you some long johns for Christmas."

Frankie waited for the annihilation, but it didn't come. "That would be kind, mother," Trix said faintly. "Jeremiah, I would like to see you for a moment."

Stan wandered off to join another group of horticultural enthusiasts. Jules's grandmother stood in conquest, an undefeated general surveying the battle scene. "Jules," she said, deploying her forces, "I would like a very small glass of vermouth—you know the kind I like. Could you find some for me?"

"Certainly, Gamma," Jules said promptly. "Don't intimidate my girl while I'm gone," he added, giving Frankie a reassuring squeeze of the hand.

"Would I ever?" Mrs. Jones's mischievous expression as she exchanged smiles with Jules put Frankie at ease. When Jules was out of earshot she turned to Frankie, her voice no longer audible to

everyone in the room. "I don't act like an old ter-
ror all the time," she said, winking conspiratori-
ally. "But saying anything I damn well please is
one of the few compensations for old age, and I
intend to enjoy it. Why do you call yourself
Frankie?"

Frankie blinked. After a moment, she said, "Being called Frances makes me uncomfortable."

"Then I'll call you Frankie too." Mrs. Jones nodded decisively. She looked Frankie over approv-
ingly. "Good roomy pelvis," she remarked. "You
can have lots of children."

The red stained Frankie's face; she had a moment's heartfelt thanks that Jules wasn't there. "I—
I don't know..." she began hesitantly.

"How old are you? Twenty-seven? Twenty-
eight?" Mrs. Jones didn't stop for Frankie's dazed
answer. "Don't wait too long, now. I want to see
my great-grandchildren before I die."

"Mrs. Jones—" Frankie began.

"Call me Gamma, like Jules does, my dear. When
he was a tiny boy, he called me Gamma Ray. Got
confused because I was Grandma *J.* and Trix's
mother was Grandma *V.*" Gamma chuckled.

"Mrs. Jones—Gamma—I don't—" Frankie took a
deep breath and tried again. "Jules hasn't—"

"Hasn't he asked you to marry him?" Gamma
chuckled again. "Well, when he does, mind you
pretend it's a surprise. And remember," she added
as Jules approached with her aperitif, "don't put
off those children! Ah, Jules." She reached for the
glass and took a large sip. "I was getting thirsty.
Aren't we supposed to have any dinner? Is Trix
serving the food yet? I suppose I should have
offered to make the biscuits, but I was looking forward to a rest for a change." There was an aged

quaver in her voice now, and the penetrating quality was back. Frankie bit her lip to avoid breaking into nervous laughter. Jules's mother, who was politely shooing people toward the dining room, flushed angrily.

Jules escorted his grandmother to her seat and then took the chair next to Frankie, ignoring his mother's signals that he should sit with Sheila Madison. The momentary pity Frankie had felt for Trix faded. She could understand why Gamma took such fiendish delight in baiting her daughter-in-law. Mrs. Jones sat by her son, but her blunt remarks could be heard by everyone.

Jules turned to Frankie. "What do you think of my grandmother?" His eyes rested fondly on the spry figure beside his father.

"She's original, that's for sure." Frankie glanced at Trix, chatting graciously to those at her end of the table and trying to pretend she didn't hear her mother-in-law's remarks. "I gather that she and your mother—"

"They don't get along," he finished for her. "Trix tried to shut Gamma out when she married dad—didn't think the old lady was polished enough for the society she moved in. But dad wouldn't stand for it, thank goodness." Jules's eyes grew introspective; Frankie could barely hear his low-voiced commentary. "Gamma was my anchor when I was growing up. She's still got all her marbles too," he added proudly. "That decrepit-old-codger act is just to get my mother's goat."

"Kind of hard on your mom, isn't it?" Frankie murmured, a sense of fairness compelling her to look at both sides.

Jules's face hardened. "She had it coming," he said shortly. As clearly as if he'd flicked a switch, his mood of introspection was gone. "Despite Gamma's insinuations," he said with a polite smile, "Trix hired a very good caterer tonight. The mousse is perfect, isn't it?"

Frankie studied him for a moment. "You're as good as your grandmother at putting on an act. What is this part, the well-bred scion of the house?"

Jules had the grace to flush. "Tell you what, Frankie. I'll give you the whole gory tale of my life some other time. Right now, I'd rather be licking this mousse off your naked flesh than sitting up at the table acting hostly." He drew a deep breath. "I don't want to put on an act with you, darlin'. You're my reality. Don't forget it."

His eyes were ardent, inflaming. His voice and his words made her tremble with feverish longing. When he raised his wineglass toward her, she touched it with her own, accepting the silent pledge they made. The wine burned a cool path into the heat that consumed her. Jules found her hand and clasped it under the tablecloth, and she felt a slow promising smile begin on her face. She could no longer remember anything they'd been discussing, anything but the way they'd held each other all afternoon. She wanted him again.

"What do you think, Ms Warburton? Shall I open the window?"

With an almost physical effort Frankie pulled her attention away from Jules. Beatrix Jones was leaning toward her. Evidently they'd been having a conversation. "I—I'm afraid I didn't get that, Mrs. Jones."

Jules's mother smiled thinly. "Please call me Trix, dear. I thought you might be too warm; you were quite flushed. Please tell me if you're not comfortable."

Frankie tried to clear her mind of the sensuous fog that pervaded it. Jules didn't help. He was still caressing her hand, doing amazingly arousing things to it beneath the chaste white tablecloth. "Well, uh, Trix, I—I'm fine, really."

There was a short deadly silence. "So have you always wanted to be in electronics?" Trix clearly felt that she was making conversation with a difficult guest, but Frankie was incapable of summoning her slim social skills while Jules wreaked such havoc with her pulse.

She cleared her throat. "I have always liked tinkering with things." She managed a smile. "But I don't particularly care for offices. I usually work out of my home."

Trix smiled sweetly, but her glance down the table toward Sheila Madison was eloquent. Sheila was talking vivaciously to Grif, whose face as he watched her had softened so as to be almost unrecognizable.

Trix was shaking her head in arch confusion. "Things are certainly different now, aren't they, Barbara?" She turned to the daintily groomed matron who sat near her, and whose face wore an older, more entrenched version of Sheila's dissatisfied pout.

Barbara shrugged wearily and reached for her newly refilled wineglass. "Not really, Trix. People are still hurting and disappointing each other regularly, just as they've been since the beginning of time." She leaned toward Frankie, who observed the whole exchange quietly. "If you'll take my advice, Miss Whoever You Are, you'll stick to your computers and forget the men. Success in marriage and motherhood is too rare to count on." With a defiant toss of her head, Barbara drained her wine-

glass and looked around for one of the hired
waiters.

Trix watched through narrowed eyes. "Barbara,
dear," she began, and then shrugged helplessly. She
transferred her attention to Sheila, seated just beyond her mother, next to Grif. "Sheila, darling,
that's a sweet outfit. Where did you get it?"

Sheila was happy to play this game and began to
recount her shopping triumphs. Frankie sipped her
own wine, turning over Barbara Madison's revelations in her mind. Jules's lips at her ear brought her
back to the present.

"Remind me," he whispered, his words taking
on a tangible presence from his warm breath,
"never to come to another one of these dinners
again. They depress me immeasurably, especially
when I'd rather be alone with you."

Frankie returned the warm pressure of his hand
on hers gratefully, but her emotions were in turmoil. The elegant room, the sleek people with their
schemes and intrigues, were like one of the melodramatic TV shows she never watched. She had
nothing in common with these people.

After dinner they regrouped in the living room.
Frankie sat next to Jules, who was in animated conversation with his grandmother and his father, discussing cousins, aunts and uncles. "What about
Sarah?" Jules turned to his grandmother. "Did she
have that baby yet?"

Gamma nodded triumphantly. "I told that girl to
stop working every day. I said, 'That baby's never
going to come if you don't sit down at home and
get ready for him.' Sure enough, two days after she
quit working she went into labor and had a nine-
pound baby boy."

Jeremiah harrumphed. "Girl should have known

how to set her own priorities. I don't know why
women even try to work when they should be
looking after their children."

Gamma changed her ground with the fluency of
long practice. "That's because you've never been
stuck at home with children, Jeremiah. Some women would be better mothers if they didn't have to
do it full-time." She glanced across the room, and
Frankie saw that she watched Barbara Madison and
Trix, who stood together by the bar.

Jeremiah looked at his mother with fond exasperation. "You jump around in an argument worse
than frog legs frying." He turned to Frankie, pinning her with a keen glance. "How about you,
young lady? What would you do about working if
you also had a husband and a baby?"

Frankie felt trapped. She looked helplessly at
Jules, but he didn't get her off the hook. "An interesting hypothetical question," he said, smiling
lazily.

"I—I don't know." Resentment began to ·rise
within her. Why should these people put her on the
spot like this? Was she being questioned as some
kind of candidate for the position of Jules's wife?
She raised her chin. "In any case, it's very hypothetical, since I don't plan either to marry or have children." She thought for a moment, then conscientiously ammended her statement, as a good scientist
should. "At least, not in the foreseeable future."·

Jules stopped smiling. Gamma and Jeremiah
looked at Frankie, then at him, then at each other.

"I think it's time I said good-night to Trix."
Gamma broke the silence, gathering up her shawl
and handkerchief. "It was nice to meet you, Miss
Frankie." She leaned toward Frankie and whispered loudly in her ear, "A bit of spirit is fine, dear,

but don't overdo it." Then she straightened. "Jeremiah, will you lend me your arm?" They moved off together.

"What the hell was that supposed to mean?" Jules's voice was low and dangerous. Frankie stood up.

"I want to go home now, Jules. That is, if the inquisition is over."

Jules's mouth tightened ominously, but after a moment, he nodded. Frankie walked swiftly over to Trix, who at the moment stood with Jeremiah near the door. Gamma had disappeared.

"Thank you for having me," she said politely to both Jules's parents. "I enjoyed the dinner." *Like hell,* she added in her thoughts.

Jeremiah surprised her by shaking her hand warmly. "I'll be seeing you around the office, Frankie."

"Until the prototype work is done," she agreed, and turned to his wife. "Goodbye, Trix. Thanks again."

Trix merely smiled, her expression neutral.

Jules walked beside her silently out to the car. When they were driving toward Palo Alto, he spoke, his voice tight.

"What the hell happened to tick you off?"

"Oh, could you tell I was angry? How perceptive of you."

Jules cursed the narrowness of the road. "There's no place to pull over and have it out, so we'll have to keep driving. If you want me to get us to the flatlands in one piece, I suggest you start talking. What's wrong?"

"How could you stand by and let them interrogate me about my fitness to be a wife and mother?" Frankie let the hurt words spill out. "What am I, an applicant for a job or something? What I choose to do with my life is my affair. I refuse to let you or your family sit in judgment on it."

Jules wrenched the car around a curve. "Frankie, you misunderstood. I—"

She was too overwrought to let him continue. "You misunderstand, Jules, if you think I'm going to marry you and turn into a mindless baby machine! If you want a nice little wife and some nice little kids, you'd better go after that nice little zero Sheila Madison. You'll never get that from me!"

The road straightened out and Jules took the first opportunity to pull over. "Listen to me, Frankie!" She opened her mouth to retort and he brought his lips down on hers, stifling the sound in her throat. The kiss started out angrily and Frankie tried to squirm away, but Jules's lips changed, softening, charging her anger with a new awareness that turned it into the spark of desire. They kissed until they were breathless with wanting. Jules dragged his lips away reluctantly.

"Frankie." His voice was hoarse. "I need...we need to talk."

Frankie's body felt heavy with fatigue, despite the fever of desire that spread through her. Suddenly she wanted only to crawl into her bed, to curl up and dream quiet solitary dreams. "Jules," she said, hesitantly. "I'm not so mad anymore. I will listen, but it has to be tomorrow. I just want.... I need to go home now."

He sighed and started the car again. "All right." They drove without speaking until they reached Frankie's house. He pulled up and looked at her soberly. In the faint light from the streetlight, she could see the earnest glimmer of his eyes.

"I'll be over in the morning."

She nodded and climbed out of the car.

"Oh, and Frankie—"

Pausing, she looked back. A smile touched his face. "It'll be early, love. *Very* early."

"Forget it," she said, trying to sound light-hearted around the huge yawn that formed in her throat. "I won't be up till noon, probably."

"I'll bring breakfast." He started the car, and she turned to walk up the sidewalk. But she heard him mutter another sentence, and when she was inside, watching him drive away, she turned it over in her muddled mind. Had he really said, "I'll do anything it takes"?

6

FRANKIE THREW DOWN the spading fork and stood up to stretch, inhaling the dark moist smell of freshly turned earth. The sun was warm enough now not to require the flannel shirt she'd put on over her overalls and tank top. She tossed it down beside the spading fork and knelt again, pulling the flat of tomato seedlings toward her.

She worked swiftly, separating the seedlings and setting them in the earth. The spicy fragrance of their leaves mingled with the earthy smells, the scents of roses and honeysuckle from the nearby flower beds, the stalks of hyacinth and lilies of the valley that sheltered on the shady side of the house. She loved working in her garden.

She'd woken that Sunday morning with the first bird chorus and been unable to get back to sleep, her body remembering the pleasures of the previous day before her mind remembered the problems. A nervous elation drove her to get up and find something, anything to do. Already she'd edged the lawn, fed the roses and hoed the corn, though it was still too small to need it. Finishing up, she firmed the earth around the last tomato seedling. Collecting, cleaning and storing her tools took a little time, but she was back in the kitchen pouring an unnecessary cup of coffee by half-past ten.

She dropped into a chair to drink the coffee, and

her mind immediately started going around and around. Jules, marriage, the tender explosive excitement of their lovemaking—her body began to tense again, to demand action. Restlessly she prowled through the house, coming at last to her office-workroom.

She paused in the doorway, taking an unconscious satisfaction from the ordered chaos of the room. Computer chassis and parts were stacked on shelves. One wall was devoted to boxed collections of journals and proceedings of professional societies to which she belonged.

On a long table that served as her desk were her backup system and terminal, with a modem next to the telephone and a printer in the far corner of the room where the noise wouldn't bother her so much. A stack of printed circuit diagrams and listings concerning Jules's project caught her eye, and she remembered a point she needed to check before the PC layout went to the fabricators tomorrow morning.

Somewhere in her card file was the phone number for the mainframe computer at Jones Morton. She switched on her system and dialed the computer, using her modem to connect her to the computer and access its files. She typed in a request for the file of algorithms that needed editing, and began paging slowly through the lines of numbers, checking them against the notations she'd made on her listing. She was nearly finished when her screen cleared unexpectedly.

"Now what?" Perhaps it was a dip in power. Before she could redial the mainframe, a message came up on the screen.

"What are you doing up so early, gorgeous? How about a date?"

"Good grief," Frankie muttered, reading the words. Maybe it was a hacker amusing himself by playing around in the files. Indignant, she typed the message code and a crisp "Who are you, anyway?"

"Captain Nemo," was the prompt reply. Frankie began to grin. Quickly she saved her work and asked for a list of current users. Sure enough, Jules's name was among the list of people working on the computer that morning, as was her own.

She sent a message to Jules. "Where's my breakfast? I'm starving!" and got back the quick reply, "So am I, but not for food." Blushing, she hoped no one was eavesdropping on their conversation. She hadn't behaved so giddily on a computer since her undergraduate days.

"So long, Captain Nemo," she typed, and waited to see what Jules would do. His reply was prompt.

"Don't jump ship. The Captain will be right over with all the goodies you can take. Au revoir."

Frankie turned off her computer and wandered around the house, in a fever of impatience to see Jules again. She hadn't forgotten the contretemps of the night before, but at the moment she could look at it more rationally. Of course Jules's father thought in terms of marriage and children. That didn't mean that she and Jules had to be tied to convention.

Thinking about children, she went into the bathroom and contemplated the birth-control device she'd procured after her first date with Jules. It seemed a bit presumptuous to use it at eleven o'clock in the morning, but she could feel anticipation rising within her, and there was no excuse for taking chances. She emerged from the bathroom protected against pregnancy, but her action, well thought out and logical though it was, provided no protection against the sudden unbidden image of Jules's child growing inside her, filling her even more completely than their lovemaking did. *Don't be stupid.* Pregnancy was no condition for a woman making her way through the world alone. Firmly she dismissed the irrational longing that had come so unexpectedly.

More restless than ever, she sauntered outside and sat on the front step, her chin in her hands. She had decided earlier that the lawn didn't need mowing, but from this angle, closer to the ground, the grass seemed pretty shaggy. She got the push mower out of the garden shed and ran it across the two small squares of lawn on either side of her front walk. There was still no sign of Jules. She took the grass catcher full of clippings back to the compost pile, her stomach growling a hungry counterpoint to her impatient thoughts.

Jules found her there, sifting dirt over the grass clippings and muttering ominously. In her faded overalls, with her hair in two long braids, he thought she looked like some ideal of the farmer's daughter. Moving silently across the grass, he came up behind her and opened the bag of warm croissants he carried, letting their delicate fragrance spill out. Frankie's nostrils flared. She quit stabbing the compost pile with the pitchfork and whirled around.

"Finally!" Despite the sharpness in her voice, her mouth blossomed into an unwilling smile. "Did you take the *Nautilus* all the way to France for them?" She seized one of the golden, flaky rolls from the bag and bit into it eagerly.

Jules showed her the other bag he'd kept hidden behind his back. "And cheese Danish. Had to visit two countries, that's why it took so long."

She looked at the sack of Danish pastries and then at the unfinished croissant in her hand. "Gosh. We're going to be really sick." Her smile broadened. "A man after my own heart. Who needs a nutritious breakfast anyway?"

"I've seen you sneaking the Twinkies out of your lunch bag," he told her, guiding her toward the back door. "What I don't understand is why you're so secretive about it."

"This is California," Frankie explained. "I got tired of hearing those lectures about blood sugar and tooth decay. Now when I need a glucose fix I eat in a corner. Why are you pushing me?"

Jules opened the door and motioned to her to enter. "I want some caffeine with my glucose." He found a cup in the cabinet and poured from the coffee maker. When they were seated across from each other at the table, he dug into the Danish bag. "Help yourself," he urged hospitably. "The cheese makes them good for you."

Frankie laughed, but took a pastry and bit into it appreciatively. "I suppose I could try scrambling some eggs or something."

Jules shook his head. "Not for me, thanks. And what do you mean, try? There's nothing particularly hard about scrambling eggs."

Frankie sighed. "Whenever I make them, they come out all dry and nasty. I really am a terrible cook."

"Hmm." He took a sip of coffee. "The coffee's all right."

"It comes in a little pack that you pour into the filter. Even I can do that." She looked across the table and took a deep breath. "You see, Jules, I'm not a good candidate for the role of executive wife."

Jules set his cup down carefully. "Now wait a

minute. Before we start slugging it out here, there's something I want to get straight.''

"And what's that?" She sat stiffly, willing herself to approach the coming argument with her usual careful logic. The problem was that she seemed to lose all her calm ability to think things through when Jules was around.

He got up and pulled her to her feet. "This, for one thing." His breath feathered her cheekbone. His lips began a trail of fire along her jaw until they fastened over her mouth. She felt the sweetness flood through her. The ache of wanting him was suddenly strong—too strong to think of resisting. She moved tentatively to brush her body against his, her hands sweeping slowly along his back. He growled and his tongue flicked out, running across her lips until they parted to let him engage her tongue in a sensuous duel. Their lower bodies arched together, the need in his meeting the want of hers. He found the side buttons of her overalls and his hands slipped inside, reveling in the firm curve of her derriere, the sleek line of back. Her breasts were round and unconfined under the thin knit of her tank top; the nipples budded at his touch, making him ache to taste them.

"Frankie," he whispered, feeling her shudder against him, "the breakfast—it wasn't enough."

"Not...satisfying?" It made his heart leap to hear the breathless catch in her voice.

"Not nearly." A ragged laugh caught in his throat. "I could take you right here...."

Her own laugh was tremulous. "Not here, not in front of the Danish!"

With her still clasped in his arms he maneuvered into the hall. "I can't see where I'm going," he mumbled against her mouth. "Can you—"

She broke loose and took his hand. "This way, sailor." He loved the mischievous smile that lit her face. She pushed him into the bedroom and shut the door, leaning against it, looking at him.

The hunger he felt to make love with her exploded inside him. He reached trembling hands to undo the fastenings of her overalls. They slid slowly to the floor, and she stepped out of them, her heavy-lidded eyes never wavering from him. She grasped the hem of the tank top and pulled it slowly over her head, tossing it aside. The thick braids of her hair fell on either side of her breasts. He took a plait in each hand and tugged gently.

Frankie went toward him willingly, feeling as if the intensity of his gaze bathed her in fire. His T-shirt had a portrait of a woman with a vaguely Victorian coiffure. "Who's this," she whispered hoarsely, tracing the woman's features with one finger.

Jules took the elastic bands off the ends of her braids. "Charlotte Bronte," he muttered, unbraiding her hair. "A very passionate woman."

"Let's get rid of her," Frankie suggested, tugging the T-shirt over his head. "And this, and this," she added, unbuckling his belt, unzipping his jeans and trying to slide them off his lean hips. He was concentrating on her hair, and finally she pushed him back onto the bed to get his clothes off. When he reached for her she jumped on top of him, letting her feminine weight move tantalizingly across the most masculine part of him.

"Love," he gasped, seizing her waist, holding her still, "I thought you realized yesterday—we can't manage this with any clothes on." He indicated the briefs that both of them still wore, and Frankie arched obligingly so that he could strip them off, first his, then hers. She maintained her advantage, however, liking the way he responded when she moved. His fingers drifted through the strands of golden brown hair that curtained her breasts, brushing it away to reveal the hard swollen nipples cresting the firm globes. His hands cupped them gently, and his mouth came up to taste each one in turn, tormenting sweetly with his teeth, until she writhed with need.

"Jules—"

"Not yet, love." His hands trailed down her body, along her quivering thighs, finding the wellspring of desire. Suddenly he moved, toppling her back on the huge old bed, kneeling between her legs, his lips playing along her stomach, his tongue finding the secrets of her inner thighs, the apex of her passion. Her eyes were shut tightly, locking her in a world of dark velvety caresses and surging rhythms.

She sent her own hands to relearn him: the ripple of muscle, the roughness of hair-covered skin, the satin-hard shaft that sought an entrance to her warmth. He groaned as she touched him and his lips came to murmur love words in her ear, his body thrusting against her, filling her with an exultation that was almost fear. She showed him the way, and they joined, their union slow and aching, full and yearning. The fear slid away as her body arched and moved, finding each moment an ever-escalating pleasure, heightened by their tongues twining hotly, his mouth on her breasts, her teeth nipping his shoulder, her hands molding his buttocks, his hands slipping between their bodies to bring her fierce delight, until finally the spiral tightened and exploded, and she grasped him hard to keep from loosing herself in the free-fall that followed.

She didn't know how long they lay together, the musky odor of their lovemaking enveloping their bodies. Finally Jules stirred.

"Either you are such a fantastic lover you make my head spin," he whispered in her ear, "or I'm having a low-blood-sugar reaction."

"I'm a fantastic lover, of course." Frankie fetched him a light clout on the arm and sighed contentedly. "We both are, come to that."

"Do you have this light-headed, sort of goofy feeling too?" He stroked her back, his fingers moving tenderly along her skin. She nodded drowsily against his chest. "Definitely low blood sugar. Time for the second course."

He rolled out of bed, and Frankie raised upon one arm to watch him. "Second course of what?"

"Breakfast, naturally." Jules put on his clothes with lightning speed. "You stay there. I'll be right back."

He left the bedroom door open when he went, and Frankie could hear him banging around in the kitchen, opening the front door, coming back in. She felt relaxed and boneless, with the quilt pulled up to her chin and the pillow fluffed behind her head. She thought about putting on her clothes, but the effort involved required more energy than she could muster.

Jules came back through the door wit[h] He'd brought a chicken-liver pâté, cris[p] smoked oysters and a bottle of champ[agne] makeshift ice bucket rigged from the [ ] double boiler. "I couldn't find the good gl[asses,]" told her, settling the tray on the bed and [sitting] carefully beside it. "But champagne from a [ ] will taste as sweet, even if it's a plastic mu[g with] Bugs Bunny's face on it."

Frankie took the mug he filled for her. "These were mine when I was little," she said with mock indignation, hitching herself up on the pillow. The quilt fell away from her breasts, and Jules smiled with pleasure.

"You look very decadent," he said, his voice soft. "Here, have some pâté."

"I feel very decadent, that's for sure," Frankie admitted. She munched the cracker thoughtfully. "Maybe there is a small degree of hypoglycemia." Everything tasted wonderful; suddenly she was ravenous again. "Are there any more Danish left?"

Jules laughed. "We'll save them for dessert." He reached forward and kissed her lingeringly, running his hands across her shoulders and down her arms. "Hey, you're cold. Why don't you get dressed and we'll go finish up your yard work."

"How can I refuse an offer like that?" Frankie shook her head in disbelief. "Not only do you cater, you do yard work too."

"Anything to keep you out of the kitchen, love." Jules busied himself with piling the remains of their feast back on the tray. "How come you're so allergic to the pots and pans?"

Frankie fastened her overalls and ran a hairbrush through her hair. "I wouldn't mind knowing how to cook, but it's a lot of trouble to learn. When I was growing up, mom and I kind of divided duties. She did the cooking, I did the cleanup; she did the marketing, I did the odd jobs." She opened the door for Jules and followed him into the kitchen. "I can fix anything that breaks—toasters, blenders, garage doors."

"You're kidding." Jules set the tray down on the counter. "Now then, show me to that shovel and

"If you're serious about helping—" Frankie began dubiously. Jules nodded and jumped around a little to show his enthusiasm. "Well, the compost pile could use turning." His enthusiasm cooled down perceptibly. "And I've been meaning to manure the melon patch."

Jules groaned, but he didn't back out. They turned the compost pile together, flexing their muscles at each other in exaggerated weight-lifter poses as they forked over the heavy stuff. Then they shoveled manure from the pile in the garden shed into a wheelbarrow for the trip to the vegetable garden.

"Is this from Manure Man?" Jules had his face half turned away from the wheelbarrow, his nose scrunched up at the odor.

"Yup." Frankie began to spread it with her shovel, moving fast. "It's not so bad," she assured him. "This is fine, well-rotted manure, not the fresh stinky stuff. It reminds me of the country around Kansas City."

"Is that where you grew up?"

She nodded assent and then, feeling pleasantly garrulous in the warm sun and the crystalline spring air, told him a little about her childhood. "Dad died when I was seven. I don't remember too much about him now. But I remember his workbench—he used to let me tighten the vise when he was making something. His hands were so big, I never understood how he could use them so delicately.

"Sounds like a good engineer."

Frankie shook her head, clearing away the sudden mist of nostalgia. "Oh, no, he was a TV repairman." She folded up the empty manure sack and tossed it onto the wheelbarrow. "Mom worked pretty hard after he died. She was a secretary during the day, and went to school at night to be an accountant." Briefly Frankie recalled the long evenings when her mother would be out at classes, or studying for them. "Now she's a CPA and makes pretty good money. She married again soon after I went to MIT for my Master's. He's a nice guy. Every year I go back there or they come out here."

"Is your mom all the family you have?"

Frankie searched Jules's face, wondering what caused the tenderness to blossom so sweetly in his eyes. "Just mom and George. Nobody else."

Jules started to say something, then bit it back. "I bet you were a proper little tomboy when you were growing up."

Frankie grinned at him. "That's my excuse for not being able to cook, anyway. Too bad I'm not going to marry you—you seem to be able to provide the groceries in a very lavish way."

Jules walked around the wheelbarrow, took the shovel from her hand and tossed it aside. He dusted off his hands and then took her chin between his finger and thumb. "Don't worry, love," he said softly, his smile disturbing. "I don't plan to ask you to marry me, so you needn't waste time turning me down."

"You...aren't going...you...."

He nodded kindly. "I know you think I was behind all my father's blathering about marriage and kids and all that dynastic stuff yesterday, but it was just because he's taken a fancy to you and thought I needed a hint. I know you don't like the idea of being tied down in marriage. I won't distress you by asking."

Frankie shut her mouth for a moment while she

marshaled her thoughts. Of course, if Jules had asked her to marry him she would have refused. But it was disconcerting to hear him say he had no intention of asking.

"I—I appreciate your concern," she said at last. "Ah, it's not exactly that I'm against the institution of marriage. I think it's fine for people who believe they're in love." Warming to her theme, she added handsomely, "Probably they don't even mind children."

"Probably not," Jules agreed, his voice polite. She glanced at him with suspicion, but his face was innocent of any hint of sarcasm.

"But I simply don't accept the concept of love." Frankie pushed the wheelbarrow back to the shed and closed the door. "The mushy kind of love, I mean."

"I know." Jules propped his shoulders against the shed and squinted into the sun. "You mean that you love your mom, and humanity in the abstract, but you don't believe you can love a man enough to spend your life with him."

"Exactly!" Frankie cried. Jules pressed his lips together and shook his head. The expression of despair that crossed his face was so fleeting she thought she'd imagined it.

"Well," he said affably, "it's all academic, isn't it? I can't stop dad from hinting around, but you'll know it's just wishful thinking on his part." He pushed away from the shed and glanced around the yard. "Neat as a pin. Is there anything else to do? No? It's a good day to try out the hot tub."

He held her hand lightly as they walked into the house so Frankie could collect her swimsuit. They talked easily together on the drive to the houseboat, interspersed with companionable silences.

The air at the marina was briny from the bay breezes, with the spicy scent of marsh grasses underlying everything. There was something very right about lounging with Jules in the warm water of the hot tub, watching boats and clouds go by, exchanging slow and secret smiles that blossomed, when at last they dried each other off, into languorous throbbing pleasure on the futon. They had dinner in a little fish place near the marina, lingering over their glasses of jug wine to talk of everything under the sun. When Jules finally took her home she drifted into the house in a haze of well-being.

But an underlying disquiet set her to wandering through the rooms instead of going to bed to be well rested for work on Monday. She ended up in the kitchen, staring blankly at a shelf of Sarabeth's cookbooks. *I really should learn to cook,* she thought, then felt the red rushing into her cheeks. "What's the use," she exclaimed aloud, her voice petulant. "He doesn't want to get married." The words seemed to echo disturbingly in the kitchen. She fled to her room, where she shed her clothes hastily and climbed into bed. *I don't love him, I don't love him,* she told herself. And a good thing too. It was lucky they thought the same way about it all.

7

THE PROTOTYPE PRINTED CIRCUIT CARD lay encased in bubble wrap, its integrated circuit chips glittering like new-wave jewels. Frankie's hands trembled slightly as she unwrapped the card and plugged it into her computer chassis. She glanced up at Jules, who hovered with barely concealed anxiety.

It was more than a week since Jules had helped her turn her compost pile and dropped that bomb about not meaning to ask her to marry him. During the days they worked hard; during the night they loved each other. But Frankie found her spare moments oddly occupied by speculation about his motives for not wanting matrimony.

There was no time for puzzling over it at the moment. This morning the prototype had come from the fabricators, and they were going to test it for the first time. Jules paced around the small office while Frankie adjusted the card carriers and fussed over the cables. "Can we get on with it?" He shoved his hands into his pockets and glared at the computer. "About this time in the debugging process, I wonder why I thought the whole thing would be worth the trouble," he muttered.

Frankie hit the "on" switch of her computer. It hummed to life, and the tiny red LED lights on the prototype board obediently lit up. She let her breath go, only then realizing that she'd been holding it.

Suddenly there was a small, distinct popping noise and an acrid odor filled the air.

"Smoked it!" Frantically she turned the system off. Jules looked at the faint puff of smoke that lingered over the backplane.

"Why?" His voice held resignation. "Why are there always problems with the prototypes?"

Frankie pulled the damaged card carefully from the backplane and laid it on her desk, reaching for the schematic that went with it. "Because they wouldn't be prototypes if they worked perfectly." She pored over the card, checking it against the schematic.

"What fried?" Jules leaned over her shoulder, his breath warm on her neck. She tried not to let it distract her from the job at hand.

"Don't know yet. Could have been the power supply, or one of the integrated circuits might be plugged in backward." She scrutinized the tiny chips and finally tapped one. "That's the culprit." She freed the prongs from the socket that held the chip to the board and held it up to the light. "Its goose is cooked, all right."

Jules took up the schematic. "So what happened? Are the traces too close?"

Frankie wrapped her arm around his waist and studied the diagram with him. "Probably. I hate to say I told you so—"

"Yeah, yeah, don't rub it in." Absently he moved his free hand up and down her side, sweeping from the sensitive flesh at the side of her breast to the curve of her hip. She shivered and snuggled closer. "So what do we do now?"

"Well...." Frankie swallowed and forced her mind to the problem. "If you added another layer, the traces would be farther apart."

Jules tossed the diagram on the floor and hugged her tightly to him. "I meant," he breathed in her ear, his hands cupping the roundness of her derriere, "what do *we* do now?" His hips moved suggestively against hers, sending a rush of desire through her.

"Jules," she murmured reluctantly, "this is an office. In here we work, remember?" She glanced at the door, which was closed—luckily, since Jules was slipping his hands under her T-shirt, bringing his palms up to cradle the aching roundness of her breasts. His lips brushed across her cheekbones, seeking her mouth. She moaned as he found her lips, at the same time gently rubbing his thumbs across the hard buds of her nipples.

"Jules, please...." She meant to protest, to draw away, but instead she melted toward him, wanting to assuage the need that was building intolerably inside her. She moved her hips in a provocative circle against the hard bulge of his pelvis, loving the way he lost control, the way he held her fiercely and thrust his tongue deep into her mouth, as if their mouths were making love the way their bodies wanted to.

"Almost lunchtime," he groaned in her ear. "Your place or mine?"

"Mine's nearer," she whispered. She pulled a little away from him. "And after lunch we debug that board."

He laughed, rubbing his cheek against her hair. "I love it when you give me that sexy tech talk. Debug the board! I've never had anybody ask me to do that with them. Does it involve mirrors or chandeliers...."

She licked her lips and made her voice husky. "No, big guy. First you take a probe—a long hard probe." Jules shook with laughter. She half closed her eyes, trying to look sultry. "Then you plug it in, very firmly, to the logic analyzer." She emphasized her words with a movement of her hips that brought his arms even tighter around her. "Then you move the probe, very slowly, all over the board—"

"Oh Lord, Frankie." His eyes gleamed with laughter and desire. "I can hardly wait. C'mon!" He pulled her out the office door and through the corridor, walking with long strides that had her half-running to keep up. They drove his Morris over to her house, since Frankie had ridden her bike to work that morning. She teased him all the way there by talking like an X-rated technical manual, and once they were naked on her bed he insisted on going over her body with his lips and hands inch by inch.

"Jules, please—"

"Got to…debug your…love circuits," he told her, his voice a heady rasp of pleasure. "You said it, *very* slowly." His lips trailed down her stomach, his tongue tasting, teasing. At last he moved over her, one hand between her thighs finding his goal, making her shudder with longing. "Probe ready," he whispered in her ear. She arched to meet him as he thrust, and together their heightened senses spiraled, taking them further and further into their private domain of ecstasy.

Afterward they helped each other dress, their busy hands creating tumescent disorder wherever they touched. Laughing, Frankie finally put a stop to the love play, pulling Jules's T-shirt over his head and pushing him off the bed. As she zipped her jeans she studied the face on his T-shirt; it looked familiar.

"Say, isn't that Lee DeForrest, the guy who invented the vacuum tube?"

Jules cast his eyes to heaven. "Shakespeare she doesn't know, Charlotte Bronte leaves her cold, but she gets DeForrest right off the bat!"

"I have my priorities," Frankie replied, unmoved. "Jones Morton started out in vacuum tubes, didn't they?"

Jules nodded. "I got my dad a T-shirt like this, but the poor guy never gets to wear it when Trix is around. She frowns on the tieless and the jacketless."

Frankie remembered that Jules had been conspicuously casual both times they'd gone to his parents' house. "And you love to rile her up," she said, frowning as they walked into the living room. "How come you two don't like each other?"

Jules's face hardened, but after a moment he shrugged. "You might as well know," he said. "There's nothing too complicated about it. My mother didn't really want children, although she didn't admit it at first. She didn't like bearing them, and she didn't know how to integrate them with the entertaining and traveling that she enjoyed. I was lucky—she simply turned me over to Gamma at an early age and went her way. My little sister wasn't so fortunate."

"I didn't know you had a sister."

He walked impatiently around the room, then opened the front door as if desperate for fresh air. "Let's get going," he growled, stepping out onto the porch. "We can continue this in the car."

He didn't head back to the industrial park right away. Instead he took a road that wound up into the foothills, driving slowly around the hairpin curves. "My sister Irene lives in Colorado now, out from under the thumbs of Trix and dad." He glanced at Frankie. "They wanted different things for her, but the result was the same—intense pressure. She's fine now. Her husband has a small electronics company and she's the controller, in her spare time from entertaining her own little daughter."

"So you're an uncle." Frankie dropped the comment uneasily into Jules's brooding silence. She had the feeling that she didn't really want to hear the story of his sister, but she also sensed that he needed to talk about it, that something had been seething inside him too long.

"Yeah. I went out at Christmas to visit—little Jennifer sure is cute. Anyway, Irene was my mother's baby doll. Trix dressed her up and took her around— wanted her to be the perfect little brainless debutante, like Sheila Madison." Jules snorted. "Irene has a real head for figures. She could certainly give Grif a run for his money. But dad didn't seem to realize that his little girl would want to be part of Jones Morton. That dubious honor was reserved for me. He let Trix take charge of Irene." Jules gave an unamused bark of laughter. "What a disaster!"

He was silent again for so long Frankie thought he had forgotten she was there. They drove through the gate of Foothill Park, and he steered the car to one of the scenic-view parking areas and stopped. "So what happened," she prompted finally.

He glanced at her and smiled grimly. "When she went away to college, Irene simply rebelled. She got in with a wild group, did a lot of drugs, got burned out. Needless to say, Trix was horrified. This long-haired, weirdly-dressed hippie wasn't *her* pretty little sweetheart. They pulled her out of Berkeley, but she wouldn't come home. At one point dad was blustering about hiring one of those deprogrammer types to drag his baby back to her cage."

He sighed and bowed his head on the steering wheel for a moment. "I wasn't much help," he admitted, his voice muffled. "I was rebelling on my own account by simply immersing myself in computers, poetry, art—anything to take the taste of money out of my mouth. I didn't emerge from my cocoon for anything except holidays with Gamma and month-long backpacking trips. I knew Irene was in trouble, but I didn't know how to help her."

He smiled fondly. "And as it turns out, she didn't need any help. She cleaned up her act, got her CPA, got married to a great fellow, but without any support from Trix, because none of it was what she wanted for her little darling. To this day, I don't think Trix has ever visited or seen Jennifer. She doesn't mention Irene if she can help it. Dad's not so bad. He went to Colorado a couple of months ago. But he couldn't help getting into a brangle with Irene about the fact that she still works for Jon's company even though she's a mother."

"He does seem to have a bee in his bonnet about working mothers," Frankie admitted, remembering his questions to her the night of the dinner party.

Jules shook his head. "I don't know why he clings to this idea that the only good mother is a full-time one. It sure didn't work with Trix. But then, he doesn't admit that, because he'd have to reevaluate his belief that it's us, Irene and me, that are at fault. As it is, he can grumble and complain, and give all his affection to Grif with a clear conscience. We tried, by gum! But we just didn't measure up."

Frankie winced at the bitterness in his voice. She

put her hand hesitantly on his shoulder, feeling a compelling need to heal, to help. "You're wrong, you know," she said, clearing her throat. "Your dad is really proud of you. He just doesn't know how to show it to his own son."

Jules looked at her in disbelief. "I don't know where you dug this fairy tale up, but it certainly won't fly. If he's so all-fired proud of me, why's he grooming Grif for the presidency of Jones Morton?"

"How do you know he is?"

"It's obvious, isn't it? Grif's his right-hand man—goes to all the meetings, makes important financial decisions. Besides, Grif has very kindly informed me of it himself." This time the bitterness was transformed into vitriol.

Frankie didn't like seeing Jules's face with that expression contorting it. "Well, I don't believe your father is going to hand Jones Morton to Grif over your head," she said briskly. "But he can hardly boot him out. I mean, Grif is the son of a founder, just like you are, you see?" It was clear that Jules wasn't listening to her. Gripping the steering wheel, he stared out over the vista of hills and blue horizons, not seeing the beauty of the scene. She touched his arm and he jumped.

"I'm sorry," he muttered, taking her cold hands in his. "I didn't mean to unload the family horror story on you. But you did ask, you know."

"It was very interesting," Frankie said truthfully. "Sort of like those TV melodramas, you know?" She was rewarded by Jules's wry smile. "But just because Trix was a lousy mother doesn't mean she's all bad, you know. Parent-child relationships are often stormy. I had terrible fights with my mom when I was in my teens. But now we're good friends, not just mother and daughter."

"You think I should try being friends with Trix?" He laughed harshly. "I don't have any respect for her or her habit of interfering in my life." He took a deep breath and fixed her with eyes full of intensity and pain. "When I was ten—I guess Irene must have been eight—Trix had an abortion. She didn't tell anyone she was pregnant, not even dad. She just flew down to Mexico for a little vacation and came back all fixed up. Dad found out somehow." He laughed again, a sound without mirth. "The fight was so loud I had no trouble figuring out what had happened. Can you imagine—without one word to anyone, to take that unborn child's life?"

The story was chilling, certainly. But against her will, Frankie felt her heart go out to Jules's mother. "It was a difficult choice to make, certainly."

"Difficult?" He pulled his hands away from her and stared at her belligerantly. "There isn't any choice in such a situation. At that time it was legally wrong. Besides, my dad deserved at least a chance to make his own preferences known. That should have kept her from doing it."

Frankie clasped her hands around her arms, shivering. Despite the bright sunlight, there was a cool breeze blowing on top of the hill. "You've said your mother was very bad at mothering," she pointed out, trying to speak calmly, to defuse the tension that filled the car. "Surely she knew she was no good at it. Why should she want to bring another child into the world to make miserable? I know—" she held up her hand to stop Jules from interrupting her "—you believe she had no right to do what she did. But try to look at it from her point of view—that of a woman for whom children are a burden and a source of pain."

Jules turned away but Frankie wasn't finished. She caught his arm and turned him back to face her. "What if you, right now, had to go through a pregnancy, have your body endure an uncomfortable and sometimes fatal experience, and be saddled with the responsibility of a baby at the end of it? Would you stop your work to care for the child? Would you spend the next twenty years of your life trying to turn it into a good human being? Or would you pass the responsibility for that on to someone else?" Aghast, Frankie stopped, aware that her voice had become high and shrill. "I didn't mean to harangue you," she whispered. "I—I think it's time we got back to work."

They didn't speak on the way back to the industrial park. Jules drove with silent, firm-lipped concentration. Frankie thought, from glances at his profile, that he was doing the same thing she was doing—continuing their argument in his mind. For herself, she was uncomfortable as Trix's champion, but no matter how much she personally disliked the woman, she felt that Jules's single-minded enmity for his own mother was unhealthy. After all, Trix had merely been exercising freedoms that women now thought of as their right—the freedom to decide what happened to their own bodies, the freedom to be something other than mothers. She had, in Frankie's opinion, misused those freedoms, but that didn't detract from her right to have them.

They parted in the hall across from Frankie's office, each of them grave and formal. It was hard to settle down to work, but she wrenched her concentration onto the problem of the prototype card's failure, and soon was engrossed, oblivious to outside influences. After three hours of painstaking work she finally found the broken trace that had caused the failure of the memory chip.

"Eureka!" Like many technical people, she had long ago formed the habit of talking to her equipment—a habit that was impossible to break. "Now let's see," she muttered, scraping away at the card and patching the trace with a temporary bridge. "Aha, my proud beauty." Unconsciously her voice assumed the melodramatic villian's accent. "We will put you back together and if you don't work—"

A voice spoke behind her, causing her to jump in startled surprise. Her hand holding the soldering iron jerked, and her temporary patch became a viscous blob of solder, oozing over everything for millimeters around.

The voice was Grif Morton's. "How are you doing, Ms Warburton," he said, his emphasis on her last name very pronounced. "I stopped in to see if your project is on schedule."

Frankie regarded him stonily. "Things are fine, thanks for asking, Mr. Morton. I am busy, see you later."

He didn't budge. "According to the rather incomplete report I've received, you're behind in your production schedule. Behind schedule means overbudget. We don't like things to run overbudget here at Jones Morton."

"I don't think," Frankie said, keeping her voice level, "that you should be talking to me about this. Jules is the project leader."

Grif was unmoved. "I preferred to talk with you, however. Jules is sometimes a little slow to see where the advantage is."

Frankie's eyebrows rose. "And you think I won't be? Think again, Mr. Morton. I'm only interested in doing my job here, as well as I can. That's all I care about."

"Hardly all." His voice was still cold, but the insinuation wasn't lost on Frankie. She reddened, and his opaque eyes took it in. "I see you know what I mean, Ms Warburton. If you care for Jules as well as your work, you ought to persuade him not to get in my way."

Frankie searched for something wounding to say. "I'm sure Jeremiah Jones will be interested in hearing what you've just told me. Would you like me to tell him for you?"

Grif moved toward her. "Jeremiah and I have an understanding," he said. He towered over her as she sat at her desk. "I am going to the top." He went to the door and paused. "And there's only room up there for one. The sooner Jules gets that message, the better for everybody."

He went through the door, and Frankie recovered from her temporary paralysis. She hurtled out of her chair. "Don't forget what they say about the top," she yelled after him. Grif paused on his way down the hall, but he didn't turn. "It's a long way down from there, and an easy fall," she added more quietly, and had the satisfaction of shutting the door carefully before he could make any comeback.

But for a long time she couldn't settle back to work. Refusing to admit to herself how much Grif's sinister chat had unsettled her, she told herself it was, after all, normal to leave work at 5:00 P.M., and she might as well depart for the day. But before leaving she put the prototype board and the schematics in her briefcase, and carried them out the door with her. Grif seemed more than ordinarily interested in the prototype. There was no sense in taking chances.

She strapped the briefcase on behind her seat and bicycled home, letting her mind think of nothing more pressing than how to negotiate the next traffic light. Sarabeth was just driving up when she arrived at her house.

"Long time no see!" Her roommate waved and waited on the doorstep till Frankie had put her bike away. "What are you doing home so early?"

Frankie shrugged. "Got burned out at the office. Thought I'd work at home tonight." She smiled at Sarabeth with pleasure. "The housemother is going to get you. You weren't home this morning when I left."

Sarabeth unlocked the door and led the way inside. "I stayed at Desmond's last night," she admitted. "Just didn't want to let the evening go somehow." She sighed.

Frankie sighed too. "Yeah, I know."

Sarabeth looked at her curiously but said nothing until they were sharing canned soup and grilled cheese sandwiches at the kitchen table. "Sounds like you're getting really involved with this Jules," she began casually.

Frankie scraped a burned spot off her sandwich and took a bite while she tried to decide how to answer. "You could say that," she hedged.

"Well?"

"Well, what?" Stirring her soup, Frankie stared at the flaccid white letters that dotted its surface. An *a*, two *c*'s, and an *x* were clearly visible. Caxc? Xacc?

Sarabeth pushed her paper plate away and captured Frankie's eyes. "If you don't want to talk about it, that's all right," she said quietly. "But I can tell something's bothering you. Want to tell Aunt Sara what it is?"

"Well...." Frankie was not used to confiding. But at last she abandoned the alphabet and plunged into a brief history of the past ten days—from the softball game that had ended their feud to Grif Morton's unsavory behavior. Sarabeth listened intently, asking a question to clarify occasionally, but letting Frankie wind down before she made any comments.

"You say you're not in love with him," she began. "How do you know?"

"Don't be silly, Sarabeth." Frankie jumped up and carried her dishes over to the sink. She threw the paper plate in the trash and turned to face her roommate again. "I don't fall in love. I like him a lot, I feel close to him, but I just am not in love with him."

Sarabeth raised her eyebrows skeptically. "Frankie, honey," she said, her Texas accent lending her words gentle emphasis, "you sound like you have love all figured out—so much of this, so much of that. But nobody has love figured out. It isn't cut and dried, you know. It's unexpected and exhilarating and incomprehensible. And sometimes you don't know you're in love until it's too late."

Frankie swallowed. "Too late?"

"Until he's gone. He won't stay around forever without a commitment from you."

They were silent for a moment. "What makes you think I want him around forever?" It was an attempt at bravado, and they both knew it. "We— we're always fighting! He's stubborn and pigheaded and won't listen to anyone else's side of the story. I tried to show him a different perspective on that whole thing with his mother—would he listen?"

Sarabeth handed her a tissue, and Frankie realized for the first time that there were tears in her eyes. She wiped them away angrily. "Honey," Sarabeth said, "your reasoning was fine, but you sounded like a logic exercise! He probably thought you should be on his side, not weighing up motives and morals. How would you feel if you told him what Grif insinuated about the two of you and he said very mildly that from Grif's point of view it was a reasonable comment?"

"He wouldn't say that!" Frankie cried passionately. "He'd—he'd probably wipe the floor with that wimp! That's why I'm not going to tell him."

"He'd be spittin' mad on your account," Sarabeth pointed out. "That's because he's in love with you."

"He doesn't want to marry me," Frankie whispered, the words coming unbidden to her lips. She looked down at the linoleum, part of her writhing at this show of emotion, part of her clamoring for reassurance. "If he loved me, he would't take no for an answer."

Sarabeth snorted in exasperation, but put a comforting arm around her shoulders. "Few men are masochistic enough to keep asking for rejection," she said wisely, steering Frankie into the living room and settling her in the most comfortable chair. "If you decide you love him, if you want to marry him, you'll just have to ask him."

"Oh, no—"

"What's the matter? A little actual liberation too much for you?" Sarabeth smiled, but her words struck home. Frankie pulled herself together and returned the smile.

"We'll see, won't we?" She turned the conversation. "What about you, Sarabeth? Are you in love with Desmond?"

"Honey," Sarabeth exclaimed, "I love them all! But it never lasts." She shrugged her slender shoulders. "Gradually, I fall out of love with them. Sometimes they even fall out of love with me."

Frankie shook her head in bewilderment. "But how can you stand it? Doesn't it hurt? To let someone you love go away—I don't see how you could ever love again."

Sarabeth looked at her keenly. "Of course it hurts," she said, her voice quiet. "So does life, when you really live it. And it's wonderful too—if you let it be. The bigger the hurt, the more it's been worth it."

"That's sick." Frankie pounded on the overstuffed arm of her chair. "Asking for hurt is, well, you said it earlier, masochistic."

Sarabeth smiled tolerantly. "Honey child, it's not asking for hurt—it's accepting it, overcoming it, that's important. If you never hurt, you're numb. And when you're numb you can't feel anything— love, or pain, or joy, or sorrow." She got up and stretched. "Computers," she pointed out gently, "don't feel anything, of course. But then, they're not alive, are they?"

Frankie stared at the geometric border on the old Persian rug that covered the floor, and let her roommate's words sink in. Sarabeth left to put on her leotard for her nightly yoga ritual, but Frankie stayed sunken in her chair, her mind rushing dizzily around, justifying, classifying, in a parody of its usual orderly ways. She felt dazed, confused. When Sarabeth returned and began limbering up, Frankie rose, feeling the need for solitude.

She wandered out to her garden, inhaling the sweetness of roses in the night air. Underlying her confusion was the conviction that Jules would call and make things right once again. She stayed outside until the evening chill finally overcame the sun's lingering warmth. Then she sat in her workroom, the prototype card lying neglected on the desk in front of her. Finally she went to bed empty, aching.

He didn't call.

8

THAT NIGHT Frankie had the dream.

It was a dream she had often in the first years after her father died. By the time she was twelve she'd learned to recognize the beginning of it and stop it before it started, and after that she didn't have it anymore.

Now, although in her sleep she knew it was the dream, she was powerless to stop it. Her sleeping body was paralyzed, unable to stir, to wake up, to evade the dream.

In it she was a child again, sitting beside her father on the old chintz-covered couch, his arm secure and warm around her. They were reading a book together; he was helping her with the hard words. In the kitchen her mother moved around, humming softly.

There was a picture of a birthday cake on one page of the book. Her mother called out from the kitchen that there were only six candles for Frankie's cake the next day, and she would be eight.

"I'll pick some up," Frankie's father said. Then the dream began to change, to lose its warm comforting aura and become dark and threatening. Something seemed to grow inside her, something ominous and inexorable. She tried to open her mouth, to say to her father, "Don't go, daddy, stay here with me where it's safe." The arm around her shoulders tightened, grew hard. She tried to keep herself from glancing down, but she had to. And when she did, her father's hand was a skeleton with naked bony fingers, pressing her down, down, until she felt she would suffocate, and she began to fight, to push desperately at the threat that engulfed her.

When she woke she was throttling her pillow, tears streaming down her face. Shakily she got up and found the aspirin, straightened the disorder of her bed and climbed back in. But sleep would not come. The dream had been as vivid as it was the day after her father had died in the car crash. It had opened the pain of his loss, brought long-stifled emotions to the surface. For the rest of the night she let her childhood return and wash over her.

When the sky began to brighten she got up and dressed. After one horrified look at her pale cheeks, at the dark circles under her eyes, she averted her face from the bathroom mirror. She drank two cups of coffee in quick succession and walked out to her car. The morning was overcast and misty, and she felt raw and exposed. The bicycle would make her too vulnerable. She needed the shell of her car between her and the world.

In her office she hunched over the prototype card, willing herself to lose all track of time and emotion in the logical tracking down of electronic errors. She kept her office door closed, fearing any intrusion until she had healed, concealed, the wounds of the night.

In her fever of work, she finished debugging the card before midmorning. For once she would have appreciated a difficult problem —anything to keep her busy. But every detail flowed smoothly together. The card was ready to go back to fabrication. Now she was without occupation until it returned.

On that thought, there was a knock and her office door opened. Gamma Jones stood there, nattily dressed in a dark suit with a huge orchid pinned to the shoulder. She beamed at Frankie.

"Here you are, my dear!" It was her "sharp" voice, with no trace of aged quaver. Jeremiah Jones's face loomed over Gamma's shoulder, wearing a cordial smile. "I'm having my annual tour of the business, and I understand you're doing something new and exciting in here." Her little black eyes darted inquisitively about.

Frankie summoned a pale smile. "Pretty much routine, actually," she said, with the sudden memory of Grif's icy face before her.

Jeremiah Jones had found the printed circuit board on her desk and was looking it over. "Hmm," he said. "What exactly does this do?"

Frankie hesitated. "Well...I'm just putting it together," she said finally, temporising in what she hoped was a diplomatic manner. "You'd have to ask Jules for the details of its operation."

As if she had conjured him by mentioning his name, Jules appeared in the doorway. "What do you want to know, dad?" His words were matter-of-fact, but his eyes flew to Frankie's face, as she felt her eyes riveted on him. They stared at each other for a long moment. She read anguish and need in his face, and something else that started a strange reaction within her. A fluttering, breath-hampering mixture of pain and longing filled her. She wanted to find herself in his arms; she wanted his lips on hers, making everything right again. His hand reached partway toward her and dropped again. Through the blood hammering through her ears she faintly heard Jeremiah Jones ask a question. Jules moved to answer it, and the spell was broken.

She took a deep breath and realized that Gamma's sharp eyes had seen the whole wordless exchange. Seen—and evidently come to some conclusion about it. The old lady took Frankie's arm in her strong, bony grip and recalled Jeremiah's attention. "We're going to the lunchroom for a cup of tea," she said authoritatively. "When you boys get through with that—" she waved her other hand dismissively toward the prototype card "—you can join us there." Bemused, Frankie allowed herself to be steered out the door and down the hall toward the small canteen that Jones Morton employees used as an informal gathering place during lunch and coffee breaks.

For an old woman who sometimes gave the impression of decrepitude, Gamma could move pretty fast. Their progress down the hall was slowed a bit by affectionate greetings from staff members who evidently knew and loved the old lady, but Gamma, although she replied in kind, didn't let anyone detain them long. Soon they were seated at a table in the canteen, deserted at this time of the morning. Frankie volunteered to get drinks from the vending machines that lined the wall, hoping to put off any disturbing confrontation. But Gamma opened fire as soon as the Styrofoam cups were on the table.

"What's wrong between you and Jules?" Somehow the expression in her eyes robbed the question of any impertinence that would have saved Frankie from answering it. But she couldn't summon up words to describe a situation she hadn't yet analyzed completely, so she shrugged and concentrated on stirring her coffee.

"Don't give me that, girl." Gamma's voice was strong and compelling. "Last time I saw you you were two little lovebirds, and now you're giving each other gloomy looks. Who's fighting—you or him?"

Frankie tried to find an answer. "Neither of us, both of us. I don't know." Then, resentment filling her voice, she burst out, "Why does everyone keep butting in? Why don't they just leave us alone?"

Gamma took it in good part, raising an eyebrow as she fished the tea bag out of her cup. "If you're talking about me, girl, I'm too old to hold my tongue anymore. And it hurts to see two youngsters that belong together botching it up." She paused for a moment. When Frankie didn't speak, she prodded, "Why don't you tell me about it? I'm good at giving advice, and I won't even nag you when you don't follow it."

Frankie smiled reluctantly. "You won't pass it on to anyone?"

Gamma looked faintly offended. "I'm not a gossip, dear. Loose lips sink ships."

Reassured, Frankie took a gulp of the lukewarm coffee. "It's—well, Jules told me about his mother—about Trix's—" She stopped for a moment, only then realizing that Gamma might not know about the abortion.

The old lady prompted her gently. "Trix's what?" When Frankie didn't reply, she frowned for a moment. "I bet it was about that little trip to Mexico," Gamma muttered. "Don't worry, child, I know all about it. That really washed Trix up in Jules's eyes, I know. It was too hard for a child to understand."

"He doesn't even try to," Frankie exclaimed. "I tried to make him see...."

Gamma was shaking her head. "I'm afraid Jules

has always been a little that way. It's not that he puts people on pedestals. But he doesn't allow those he loves to make many mistakes. Step out of line too often, and—" She ran her finger over her throat in graphic pantomime.

"Well, who gets to decide where the line is?" Frankie banged the table, sloshing some of her coffee onto the Formica top. "I mean, even in Trix's case—"

"It wasn't all her fault, anyway." Gamma spoke with reluctance, as if determined to play fair no matter how distasteful it would be. "I told Jeremiah back then he had only himself to blame. A man who spends all his time nursing his business along and leaving the raising of his children totally to his wife deserves what he gets. It wasn't as if he didn't know Trix was a silly little fluff head. He knew *that* before he married her."

Frankie was too fascinated by these revelations to obey the voice inside her that told her to change the subject. "Why did he marry her then?" she asked instead, feeling faintly ashamed of herself for asking.

Gamma looked at her for a moment, measuringly. "He got her pregnant," she said finally. "Her family went into a tailspin—they were an old Atherton name—had a lot of experience hushing up scandal." She snorted. "I told him to do as he felt right, so he married her. The question is why she wanted to marry him, but I guess her family pressured her to take the easy solution." She leaned forward and laid a hand on Frankie's arm. "Don't tell Jules. I don't know if he knows it or not, but he's just enough of a fool to feel to blame for causing the mismatch of the century."

Frankie nodded in abstracted agreement. It was

vaguely comforting to know that someone else
agreed with her, but it didn't really help any in re-
conciling the differences between Jules and her. In
fact, she began to worry about the implications of
some things Gamma had said. Would Jules regard
her meddling in his feelings for his mother as stepping out of line?

Gamma touched her hand again. "I know I
haven't been much help, dear. Believe me, I want to
see things prosper between the two of you. Jules
needs a *real* woman like you."

Frankie blinked. "I'm a *real* woman?" She thought
of Sheila Madison's pretty, well-made-up face. "You
could fool me."

This time it was Gamma who banged her fist on
the table. "Now, girl, I don't want to hear any of
that. A woman isn't just what's on the outside. It's
the inside that counts through the years." She
thumped her own chest. "The reason why I'm such
a great person at my time of life is what's inside me.
The outsides have long since started going to pot."

Frankie smiled teasingly. "I don't want to hear
any of that." After a moment she added, "Thanks
for the compliment."

They were silent for a moment. "So something
else is puzzling you, dearie. What is it?"

Frankie had been thinking about the other source
of friction that had surfaced at Jones Morton. She
couldn't keep from blurting out a question that had
been bothering her since the previous afternoon.
"Does—does Jules's dad intend to put Grif in the
presidency when he retires?"

Gamma looked at her, her gaze revealing nothing. "Now I wonder why that's important for you
to know," she said finally.

Frankie blushed, only then realizing the imputation that could be put on her question. "It doesn't matter to me," she cried. "But Jules—it's eating away at him. And Grif—" she stopped, unwilling to pass along what Grif had said.

Gamma's face relaxed. "I suppose Grif has been taunting Jules with it. The same old story." She sighed and patted Frankie's hand. "Don't worry, my dear. Jeremiah thinks very highly of Jules's work. You can rest assured that he will get what he wants." She must have read the doubt that her equivocal answer raised in Frankie. Her voice went up. "Believe me, my dear, I wouldn't stand by and see my only grandson slighted."

"Yes, but—" Frankie shrugged eloquently. How much could one old woman do, no matter how game she was?

"I guess you don't realize that I hold an equity position in Jones Morton," Gamma said, chuckling comfortably at Frankie's expression of surprise. "Yes, indeed, when my boy was looking for capital to start up with Stan Morton, I put in all the insurance money I'd gotten after Justin, my husband, died. Jeremiah didn't want to take it, said he didn't want to rob the widows and children. But I insisted. My old-age pension, I called it. And now—" she patted the sleeve of her elegant suit with a complacent smile "—I can please myself about most anything that involves money. Too bad that's such a small part of life."

"That's great, Mrs. Jones."

"Call me Gamma. Everyone else does."

"Gamma, then." Frankie smiled in true affection, liking the gallant way Jules's grandmother looked at things. "But if you have that kind of power here—" she couldn't keep the doubt from creeping into her voice "—why don't you set Jules's mind at ease? And if Grif's not going to be president, it seems cruel to let him expect that he is.''

"Now, now." Gamma looked slightly alarmed. "You must realize, my dear, that nothing is settled. It will be a few years before Jeremiah's ready to retire. The best thing for both those boys is to do their work the best way they can and not go putting carts before horses." She gave Frankie a sharp look. "I hope you realize I wouldn't talk like this to just anyone."

Frankie smiled, understanding where Gamma's concerns lay. "Believe me, Gamma, you will be the first to know if anything interesting develops between Jules and me." Impulsively she grasped the old lady's hand, feeling as if some of the angst with which she'd started the day was melting.

There was no time for further confidential talk. Jules and his father joined them. Jeremiah was in a boisterous, backslapping mood, greeting Frankie with a ribald wink and bestowing a gruff accolade on Jules's design work. Jules, Frankie saw, was less convivial. He replied to every remark addressed to him, but his eyes remained on Frankie, brooding and intense. It was too unsettling to endure that scrutiny; Frankie fixed her own eyes on the dregs of coffee in her dented Styrofoam cup, and fell silent.

Gamma finally chirped, "Well, son, time for that wonderful lunch you promised me." Her voice changed slightly. "Are we meeting Trix?"

Jeremiah cleared his throat. "No, she had a charity luncheon to attend today." He turned to Jules. "Perhaps you and Miss Frankie would like to come with us."

Jules didn't answer at once and Frankie jumped in, her voice slightly unsteady. "Sorry, I'm not dressed for going out to lunch. But you all have fun."

Jeremiah started to protest, but stopped—probably, Frankie thought, with a wild urge to giggle, because Gamma had stomped on his foot under the table.

"These two young things will want to talk over their work," she said, staring meaningfully at Frankie. "Let's get along, laddie." With Jeremiah's help she rose from her chair and came around to lay her hand against Frankie's cheek. "Such a pretty young thing," she said, her manner reverting to her "decrepit" act. "Mind you spend your youth the right way." She hobbled out on her son's arm.

Jules stared after her, a puzzled frown on his face. "What did she mean by that crack, I wonder." He turned his gaze on Frankie, who blushed and fiddled with her cup.

"Probably she was just wandering." She tried to keep her voice airy, unconcerned.

"Gamma has never wandered in her life unless it suited her purpose," he muttered. She stole a look at him and realized that he'd dismissed his grandmother from his mind. Once more his eyes were fixed on her with burning eloquence.

"Frankie," he began, obviously choosing his words with care. "I—I overreacted yesterday. Please, let's not fight about things that don't matter to us."

"Don't they?" Frankie's voice was low. The same feelings of panic and loss that she'd had during her dream the previous night loomed inside her. Fear filled her—fear that she would never have the closeness with dear ones—something others took for granted—fear that she was doomed somehow to a lifetime of withdrawal because of her father's untimely death. She clutched Jules's hand.

"What is it? What's wrong?" Jules felt his ambivalence toward the situation with Frankie swept away by the imploring urgency in her eyes. How could she change so suddenly from her usual stance of sturdy independence? "Frankie, love—"

"I want to be with you," she said, her voice intense. "I want to make love with you now. Please, Jules—"

He shook his head helplessly. "I don't—"

She took his hand and pulled him from the table. "Let's go to your place."

They drove silently in Frankie's little station wagon, Jules sitting in the passenger seat with his arms crossed. It was a different sensation to be swept away by a woman's passion and need, to have her take charge of the experience. He wanted to see how far it would take him. For a little while he was caught by the novelty, by projecting scenarios of role reversal. But one glance at Frankie's set profile made him wonder about her reasons for dragging him away, more or less by his hair. "This is very flattering," he began cautiously.

She glanced at him before returning her eyes to the road. "It's not meant to be flattering."

He cleared his throat. "Then what is it meant to be?" She didn't answer right away. He thought he could almost see the wheels going around in that logical brain of hers, and then he knew that she was acting on impulse—for her, he guessed, a rare experience. He added, gently teasing, "I hope you're not going to just use me and toss me away." As soon as he said the words, he had the desolate feeling that she meant to do exactly that.

She examined his words and finally smiled. "I

won't toss you away," she promised, pulling into his parking spot at the marina. She started off down the dock without waiting for him and he followed slowly, admiring the way her golden-brown hair caught the sun and threw it back. She looked cute from the rear. Anticipation grew within him.

She was waiting at his door, not quite bouncing up and down with impatience. He let her in and stood beside the door, watching her.

As if his scrutiny made her uneasy, she moved aimlessly around the small room, touching the shiny polished brass of the barometer, running her hand along the sleek mahogany surface of a cupboard. Finally she stopped for a moment, then came to stand in front of him. Still he made no move.

"Jules, are you...reluctant? Is this a bad idea?" Her words were wistful, half whispered. A smile tugged at his mouth.

"No, love."

"Well...why are you just standing there?"

He let his eyes caress every inch of her face, let the emotion well up within him. "What do you want me to do?"

She licked her lips and returned his stare with growing confidence. "Um...." Her voice was still a whisper, but husky now, sending a message. "You could try taking off your clothes."

He pulled his T-shirt off and let it drop to the floor, keeping his eyes fixed on her, feeling his blood heat as her expression changed. "Wait," she breathed as his hands went to his belt. Her own shirt joined his on the floor. Her nipples stood out, taut already; it was hard for him to resist reaching to caress them. But Frankie had the bit between her teeth at the moment. He was content to let her guide.

She came closer, and her hands found the supple flesh of his shoulders, smoothing down over his chest until her fingers touched the hard male nipples. She was watching him, her mouth slightly open, as she gently pulled the tiny nubs. Desire flared within him, and she saw it in his eyes and smiled, satisfied. Her mouth replaced her hands; then she pulled back to look at him. "Good." Her voice was almost a purr. He forced back an urge to crush her to him.

At last she was unfastening his belt, pushing off his jeans, guiding them down his legs, letting her hands find their wanton way back to his waist. His breath came fast; he felt his eyes glaze with passion as her own jeans fell to the floor. She took his hand and led him past their discarded clothing to the welcome softness of the futon.

They knelt, facing each other; their eyes locked together. He ached for her lips but she gave him only teasing, tormenting tastes that left him dazed and helpless. With infinite slowness she experimented with their bodies, fitting herself against him, rubbing her nipples across his nipples, parting her thighs to allow his hardness a teasing, intimate exploration. It was too much; it was not enough.

When at last she brought her lips to his again, he let his passion explode against her. Their tongues met in fiery battle, igniting every sensitized inch of their bodies. She cried out and pushed him over, falling softly on top of him in a furious tangle of silky arms and legs, her hair spilling like a satin curtain around their fierce intent faces. Tenderly she held his hard, throbbing need, and then moved to make it hers. He arched at the pleasure shock, finding his hands tangled in her hair, holding her to him, binding her to him.

Their lips came together again, and he realized he was whispering her name, whispering his love, in a voice that went on and on in his head even though his lips were sealed hot and wet against hers, even though their tongues were thrusting and twining in the dark cavern of their joined mouths. She pulled her mouth away with a gasp, and then his lips found her breasts. He filled his empty hands with their exquisite roundness, burying his hot face, moving his mouth blindly from one turgid nipple to the other, while she rode with fierce triumphant cries to a climax that gripped him tumultuously and made him shout hoarse, unintelligible words before he lost himself in her body, in her mind.

Frankie listened to Jules's heart slow gradually to normal beneath her ear and started to wonder what had prompted this brief interlude of sensual madness. She still tingled with the afterglow of pleasure. When Jules's hand moved in slow caresses over her breast and hip, she felt like purring. But underneath was something dark and nameless that stirred ominously.

Jules murmured gentle words into her hair, then lifted her head with a hand under her chin. "You all right, Frankie?"

She nodded, her eyes cast down, afraid for some reason to meet that penetrating stare. Even softened with love, his hazel eyes were formidably keen. She was half afraid he would question her further, but he smoothed her hair one more time and then sat up. "Shall I turn on the hot tub?"

She licked her lips. "I guess—I guess we should go back to work," she offered, hesitant.

He waved it away. "I sent the prototype board to the fabricators, since you'd evidently finished debugging it. We've been working hard. We deserve some time off." He pulled on a pair of cut-offs and disappeared on the back deck.

Frankie found the swimsuit she'd worn last time and pulled it on, suddenly needing the armor of clothes against some nebulous attack. When Jules returned she was twirling her hair into a knot on top of her head. "How long will it take to heat up?" She tried to keep her voice careless, casual, but some underlying hint of panic must have reached him.

Ignoring her question, he took her gently in his arms. "What's wrong, Frankie?"

"Why should something be wrong?" Horrified, she heard the querulous note in her voice, but was unable to repress it or to stop talking. "Didn't you enjoy making love? Was it bad for you? I'm sorry if I was clumsy or something...." She made herself bite her tongue, and closed her eyes in despair. "I really am sorry," she whispered, keeping tears at bay with an effort.

He pushed her head gently against his shoulder and stroked her back, his hands soothing. "Don't be sorry," he said. "There was nothing at all the matter with the lovemaking and you know it. It was the best ever, in this universe or any other." His hands were warm and mesmeric on her bare back, and she let herself relax and be comforted by them. "But I know something's wrong right now," he added. "If it would help to tell me, I'll certainly listen."

She opened her mouth to protest. "My father—" The words surprised her. She hadn't meant to say them, hadn't even known they were there. Suddenly she was crying, big, hiccuping sobs, the words spilling out unintelligibly. "He died—it was my birthday—I dreamed—"

Jules sat down with her on a cushion and held her shaking body, managing somehow to piece the story together from her incoherent utterances. At last she was quiet, an occasional sob shaking her.

"Have you been carrying this around all alone these years?" His voice was carefully calm. "Did you ever talk to your mother about it?"

Frankie felt too exhausted to speak, to move. She managed a tiny negative shake of her head.

"Why not?"

For a long moment she was still. Finally she moved back in his arms to look at his face. "What is this, punishment for my interference in your life the other day?"

Jules refused to respond to her antagonistic tone. "Don't be so touchy. I really want to know." He waited a moment, but she could not reply. "I can guess, you know. You obviously felt—still feel, on some level—responsible for the car accident that took your father's life, because if it hadn't been for your birthday he wouldn't have gone out. That's bull, of course, but emotions can't be ruled by whats right or wrong logically. But I bet your mother felt guilty too—she's the one who sent him out, after all. She's probably sublimated it much more successfully than you have, however. Maybe if you two talked about it you could come to grips with it all."

Part of Frankie found this pat explanation reasonable. But part of her, irrationally, clung to her long-suppressed trauma. "You can't know anything about it," she cried passionately. "You still have a father!"

Jules frowned but kept his temper. "That's right," he said softly. "I haven't managed the scars of my childhood any too well, either. Seems like we're both still at the mercy of feelings for our parents that should have been resolved long ago."

Frankie wrung her hands. The whole afternoon had overset her usual calm, logical approach to life. She felt battered, sensitive to touch unable to cope with the abrasive facts of living. "What can I do?" she cried, the anguish in her voice surprising her. "I—I don't know how to handle any of this."

Jules's voice was purposely matter-of-fact. "Come sit in the hot tub with me, love." He took her hand and led her gently to the back deck. "We'll get a few things into perspective."

"You Californians," she grumbled, although she let him guide her to the tub. "You think a hot tub will solve all the world's problems."

His lips quirked into a smile as he sat back in the warm, swirling water. "Seems to me I read something about the folks down at Esalen inviting all the world leaders for a soak and a rap about peace." He stretched his legs out and sighed deeply. "Now confess. Doesn't it feel wonderful?"

There was a part of Frankie that felt perversely inclined to disagreee with anything anyone said, but she couldn't disagree about this. The feeling of being cradled in the warm watery depths was immensely soothing to her lacerated nerves. She could almost imagine that her wounds were healing, her body renewing. "It's okay," she admitted grudgingly.

He paid no attention to this poor-spirited remark. "Now," he ordered, in a brisk voice that was at variance with his relaxed, languid appearance. "I want you to spill your guts about your childhood. Tell me the first thing you can remember ever."

Frankie hesitated, but his eyes were compelling. "The lilac bushes in the front yard," she said slowly. "They grew in a circle, and there was a space in the center. I remember sitting in it—my secret place. I had a doll named Marylou." She looked at Jules wonderingly. "I haven't thought about that in—in a thousand years! What's the first thing you remember?"

"My father laughing," he said promptly. "It was my third birthday, and I fell into the birthday cake. I remember looking out through the icing on my lashes and seeing my mother poking my father in the ribs to stop him from laughing at me." He looked faintly surprised and sat up a little straighter. "This is going to be interesting. Keep talking."

They were still exchanging memories of their very different childhoods when Sheila Madison found them. Her heels came tapping around the narrow companionway that surrounded the boat, and Jules straightened in annoyance. "Now who can this be," he grumbled, just before Sheila's perfectly made-up face peered around the corner of the boat.

"So you *are* here, Jules darling." She managed to coo at Jules and scowl at Frankie in a single sentence. Frankie pasted a noncommittal smile on her face, but resentment flowed through her. She didn't want the magic she and Jules were experiencing to end.

"What are you doing here, Sheila?" Jules made no move to emerge from the hot tub.

"I—well, I'm almost embarrassed to say." Sheila's voice was still as sweet as pie, but with her newfound empathy Frankie could detect the uneasiness beneath it. The *Nautilus*'s tiny back deck was almost

totally devoted to the tub, and Sheila had to stand
right up against the back wall of the cabin to avoid
the gentle splashing of the water whenever Jules or
Frankie moved. She was dressed to the hilt, in a
clinging outfit of some soft topaz fabric that set off
her eyes and hair. Her shoes and handbag screamed
"expensive designer." Frankie sat a little straighter,
wanting to loath her but sensing that there might be
something human about Sheila after all.

Sheila pressed closer to the wall and clutched her
bag nervously. "Actually," she began, "Trix told
me not to bother you. But I—I couldn't think of
anyone else. You know the benefit fashion show
that Trix is coordinating? Well, Billy Meyers who
was supposed to be my escort has come down with
chicken pox of all things. Can you imagine?"

Jules stirred restlessly and a couple of drops of
water dotted the expensive pumps, but Sheila
didn't notice. To Frankie, she suddenly seemed
young and insecure. "I thought you might be a
lamb and help out for the afternoon. Any dark suit
will be fine, so there's no problem with dress." She
raised her eyebrows at his submerged form with a
return of her previous manner. Jules was still clad
in the cut-offs he'd pulled on to go out and turn on
the hot tub. The shorts were molded wetly to his
lean muscular hips, and privately Frankie thought
them more becoming than any other garments he
might put on.

Jules had a resigned expression on his face.
"Sheila, you're too old now to keep running to me
to get out of scrapes. If you can't dig up someone to
be your escort, you'll just have to solo."

Tears welled up in Sheila's lovely eyes. "But
Jules," she wailed. "I was counting on you. You
never let me down!"

A sudden irrational fury filled Frankie. She scrambled from the hot tub, taking a bit of malicious pleasure at the drops of water that marred Sheila's perfect shoes. Stalking over to the towels hanging on the railing, Frankie wrapped one around her wet shivering body and groped for her usual aura of straight forward practicality, but it was hard to find. The past few hours had been among the most exalted, terrifying, enlightening moments of her life. It was too infuriating to have Sheila interrupt it and spoil it all, to have to wonder if Jules was going to fall for her old-friend-of-the-family line. Some of the rage and turmoil that had possessed her earlier came boiling to the forefront.

"Yes, indeed, you must find your dark suit," she said, her voice even. "I need to get back to the office for a while anyway. Thanks for inviting me to share the hot tub Jules."

His face, when she dared to look at it, was impassive, but she thought she could read a trace of sympathy in his eyes. He said nothing until she was at the back door.

"Frankie." His voice held all the tenderness, all the intimacy they'd shared together that day. Hearing it made her eyes prick with tears. She kept her back turned, afraid to reveal any vulnerability to Sheila's inquisitive little eyes. "I talked to Grif yesterday afternoon." He waited a moment to let his words sink in. She was a little slow in putting together the implications, but finally her mind connected Grif, his veiled innuendos to her the day before, her own reaction to them. All thoughts of tears fled. Stiffly she turned to face Jules, uncertain what she would see when she looked at him.

"He was a bit...cryptic," Jules said carefully, remembering as she did Sheila's avid ears. "But I think it would be best from now on if we worked in the tank." Then he smiled, and she saw that heart-gripping emotion offered freely, hers whether she wanted it or not. She nodded blankly and stumbled into the cabin, picking up her clothes in a daze, only realizing when she'd driven halfway home that she was still in a damp bathing suit, wearing Jules's towel. At the same time she found she could put a name to the emotion that she saw constantly in Jules's eyes. It was love.

Jules watched her disappear through the back door and sighed briefly. It was not the end he would have wished to their afternoon. But he could sense that Frankie had taken as much as she could bear of remembrance and emotional surrender. Whether she knew it or not, she needed some time alone. It would be just like her to go back to the office searching for the solitude of work, and he didn't want her exposed to any more of Grif's probing. From what Grif had let fall to him yesterday, he had a pretty clear picture of the scene Frankie had endured. If they worked in the tank from now on, a secured area of the building that took special security clearances to enter, Grif would no longer have access to them—or the prototype.

When he heard her car drive away, Jules sighed wistfully. He had never revealed as much of himself to another person as he had to Frankie this afternoon. If she didn't realize pretty soon that she loved him back, he would have to do something drastic.

Sheila recalled herself to his mind by clearing her throat gently. "Jules, darling. You will help me out, won't you? I knew I could count on you." He stared at her blankly and got to his feet. Interpreting this as acquiescense to her desires, Sheila chattered on. "Is that Miss Warburton here often? At your parents' dinner party the other day, I thought her rather odd." Jules didn't answer, and her evil genius prompted Sheila to talk on. "I do wonder, though, why women like that don't make more of an effort. She would be almost attractive if she would just pay more attention to her personal grooming."

Jules grabbed his own towel from the railing and began to dry his chest. "You are speaking," he said mildly, "of my future wife." He observed Sheila blandly while he unzipped his cut-offs and draped the towel around his waist. For a moment he almost admired her. She didn't give in to rage or hysterics. She merely blinked and politely averted her eyes while he stripped the shorts off underneath the towel.

"You're joking, of course," she assured him. "How can you think of making her Mrs. Julian Jones? Why anyone can see she knows nothing about the behavior required of a corporate wife."

And you do, I suppose? Jules found himself pitying the inevitable disillusions that would face Sheila in her life. He knew, from being saddled with her problems at intervals during his younger years, that Sheila was as strong-minded as any suffragette, under her high-gloss exterior. No point in worrying about her.

"Mrs. Julian Jones." He considered for a moment, his face grave. "You're probably right about that. I bet she'll want to retain her own name. But I'm sure she'll be amenable to exchanging rings." Sheila's mouth opened, but no words came out. To forestall anything she might find to say, he added, still without raising his voice, "As for your fashion show, I'm sure you see it's out of the question. It might make me an object of ridicule to my future wife, and that would never do." He opened the back door of the boat and paused. "See you around, Sheila," he said politely before closing the door on her distraught face.

9

THERE IS A KIND OF SHOCK that comes when the mind uncloses its secrets to itself. Frankie was numb with revelations; she could barely function at all. Clutching her clothes and the damp clammy towel, she walked up her sidewalk, immune for the first time to the beauty and lush scent of her garden. She headed for the kitchen and put on hot water for instant coffee. Sarabeth found her there a little later, still in her bathing suit, sitting at the kitchen table with the lukewarm cup cradled in her hands, her eyes fixed blankly on the window.

Sarabeth raised her eyebrows and turned the water on under the kettle. "Kind of early for swimming," she suggested. Frankie's head swiveled to regard her roommate, and Sarabeth's expression changed. "Honey, what is it?" What's happened?"

Frankie giggled inanely. "Warning. Disk full. Use escape key. Use escape key." Her voice rose. "Too bad there is no escape key. Sometimes you burn out the central processing unit...."

Sarabeth shook her gently by the shoulders. "Get a grip on yourself. Now, what happened?" Frankie tried to marshall her thoughts for a coherent explanation. "I know." Sarabeth nodded wisely. "You were seized with a sudden urge to play in the sprinkler. But first you took out your normal brain and replaced it with logic circuits, and that's why you keep giving me this computer babble."

Frankie clutched her temples. "No," she moaned. "In fact, vice versa. I replaced my logic circuits with something else—something spongy and inadequate. I don't seem to be able to think at all." She looked hopefully at her roommate. "Do you think it's a brain tumor? Maybe surgery is the answer."

Sarabeth shook her head tolerantly and went to turn off the kettle's insistent whistle. "Honey, I could make a diagnosis for what ails you, but you aren't willing to take the cure. Was Jules playing in the sprinkler with you?"

Frankie managed to be succinct. "Hot tub. His place."

Sarabeth looked impressed. "Any man who can fit a hot tub onto a houseboat has the true American spirit. So you've been frolicking in the bubbles." She eyed Frankie's suit. "Although with a certain amount of decorum it seems. What comes next?"

"Next?" Frankie glanced down at her swimsuit. "I'm cold," she mumbled. "It's too early in the year to sit around in a damp swimsuit. Damn him anyway!"

"Did he kick you out?" Sarabeth brought an apple to the table along with a cup of herb tea, and began to cut the apple into quarters. "'Begone, thou maid of mush-mind, and take thy clothing with thee'—that sort of thing?"

"Not—not exactly." Frankie tried to explain the afternoon's events to her roommate, without much success, since she couldn't explain even to herself why she had acted the way she did. Sarabeth listened impassively.

"Let me see if I have it straight now," she said, when Frankie finally ran down. "You dragged the man off to his bed. Then you had an emotional crisis all over him, something I find difficult to believe of Ms Logic Circuits. Then, after he'd given you a nice broad shoulder to cry on, complete with hot tub and intimate conversation, you ran out on him when he was in danger."

"In danger?" Frankie gulped the rest of her coffee, only vaguely aware that it was stone cold.

"In danger of being dragged off to some fashion show, and perhaps even in danger of being shanghaied for life by a young woman whom I believe you described as an animated Barbie doll." She looked at her questioningly and Frankie nodded miserably.

"I don't know what to do!" She banged her cup on the table and wrapped her arms around her shivering body. "Yes, I do," she contradicted herself immediately. "I can take a shower. You don't need a brain to take a shower. You just turn on the faucet and the water comes out."

She trailed the towel toward the door. "Remember," Sarabeth called after her, the last slice of apple poised for a bite, "you have to get *under* the shower or it doesn't do anything for you."

Frankie stayed in the shower for twenty minutes, letting the warmth of the water wash away her anxieties. When she stepped out at last, she felt a kind of calm resignation permeate her psyche. There would, she knew, come a time of reckoning. She would have to think about the events of the past few days and fit them somehow into her life. For the time being, she would move one step at a time, and avoid looking ahead or behind. For the time being she would simply exist.

She drove to Jones Morton, wanting to pick up some of the diskettes she'd left there so she could work on her backup system at home. With the fatalism born of desperation she knew she wouldn't see Jules there, and she was right. He was probably already wearing his dark suit at that fashion show. But he had left orders for her equipment to be moved into the tank, which meant that she had to arrange for a special security badge that could be used to unlock the tank's door.

Because the nature of her work took her to many high-security companies, Frankie kept her government security clearances up to date. Nan, the receptionist in the front hall, had already done most of the paperwork. All that remained was to sign in what seemed like a hundred different places on the papers.

Frankie read through them automatically, listening absently when Pamela, the secretary that worked near her office, came through the hall and stopped for a few minutes' gossip with Nan. "Looks sort of like Christopher Reeve," Pamela was saying. She turned to Frankie and asked, "Don't you think Jules looks like Christopher Reeve?"

"Hm," Frankie said noncommittally, not wanting to ask who Christopher Reeve was.

"Are you going to the poetry reading tonight?" Nan directed the question to Pamela, although her eyes slid to Frankie.

"Is he going to be there?" Pamela looked thoughtful. "John Farrigon asked me to the movies, or I might just do it." She sighed heavily. "The way he looks up there at the podium!" She giggled and drifted down the hall.

Frankie finished signing her name and took the plastic credit-card-sized badge, pinning it absently to her shirt. She carried a load of disk boxes and printouts to the tank, pushing the badge into a slot in the heavy steel door to open it. The tank was a huge impersonal space, like some kind of shrine to the machine age, where the incessant hum of equipment drowned out every other sound. Frankie's computer was already set up in one of the partitioned-off work stations. She arranged her desk and tested her equipment. But in the back of her mind she was turning Pamela's words over.

She took the diskette she needed to work at home and let herself back out of the tank, submitting to the electronic scrutiny of a sentry machine whose video screen showed a human guard, lounging in the main security complex. If she hadn't been so preoccupied with Julian Jones, Frankie would have resented this enormously, and probably vocally. As it was, she merely gave the screen a disdainful glance before hurrying back to her old office. On the bulletin board outside the door was an assortment of flyers advertising community meetings and events. Among them she found one that invited the public to the readings of the Tall Tree Poets, who met one evening a month at a local community college. She scribbled the address on one of her listings and went home, arguing with herself all the way.

Sarabeth was out for dinner. Frankie ate a solitary hot dog, still debating whether she should show up at the poetry reading and risk a case of terminal embarrassment, or whether she should stay at home longing for a glimpse of Jules.

"Don't be a sap," she told the bottle of dish detergent. "You'll look like some silly high-school girl mooning around with a crush. Be cool. The man knows where you live if he wants to see you."

"Yes," she told the bathroom mirror as she

braided her hair. "But what kind of poetry does he write? That's all I'm really interested in. What if he's written something about *me*? Shouldn't I hear it?"

She wandered into her bedroom and dabbed a little rose essence on her wrists, put on a little mascara. "My interests are too narrow," she said, addressing the picture of her mother that stood on her bureau. "I don't expose myself enough to the fine arts. This poetry reading could be good for my soul."

At quarter to eight she shrugged on a light jacket and walked out the door, locking it behind her with a feeling of burning her bridges. "I'll just drive by on my way to the market," she said virtuously to one of her rosebushes. "There won't be a place to park, anyway."

There was a place to park, right in front of the building. However, she drove around to the lot in back, not too anxious to advertise her presence.

The community college was a former office building with lots of doors opening onto a courtyard. It was easy to see where the poets were—and to hear them. From one room came a loud gaggle of voices, punctuated with frequent bursts of laughter. Frankie skulked toward the room, noticing the people who clustered around the door. Some were wearing three-piece suits, and a few were left over from the flower-child era, with flowing hair and flowing clothes. She spotted Jules's dark head bent over a lush older woman with slanting, seductive eyes. Guiltily she sneaked behind him through the door and into the shadowy back of the room, where she found a chair and dropped into it, feeling as if she were keeping some illicit assignation.

The room began to fill with people. One tall,

long-haired, bearded giant plopped down in front of Frankie, hiding her effectively from the rest of the room. She relaxed, peeking around her shield's massive form to locate Jules. He was sitting between the woman he'd been talking to earlier and another woman, a thin nervous-looking person who constantly touched his arm and talked into his ear. Frankie found that she didn't much like watching this.

A man stood at the podium—a scruffy, medium-sized fellow with a huge booming voice. Consulting a list in his hand, he called out a name, and someone would get up from the audience to read, generally quite unabashed at the presence of fifty or so pairs of critical eyes. The poems ranged from traditional ballads and sonnets to terse, almost unintelligible groupings of words. Frankie was unexpectedly fascinated. She listened intently, even to the ones that were too cryptic to understand, or too grotesque to take seriously. Some of the readers moved her.

The man at the podium called Jules's name, and Frankie felt a sudden clutch at her stomach. She had almost forgotten what she was doing here. Pamela had been right. Jules did look fine at the podium; he was relaxed, with a faint smile on his lips, as he waited for the audience to quiet.

"For those of you who might be confused," he said into the sudden stillness of the room, "this poem is a fantasy monologue that Charlotte Bronte's Rochester might have thought about his problems with Jane Eyre." Frankie noticed suddenly that he was wearing the Charlotte Bronte T-shirt again. Others in the audience evidently knew the writer's face; the murmurings didn't quiet until he began to read.

He read in a conversational, undramatic way that only made his words more emphatic. Frankie wasn't familiar with *Jane Eyre*, but she responded to the forcefulness of Jules's vision of Rochester as a man driven beyond rationality by his love for a prickly, independent, maddening woman.

Frankie felt exalted and terrified at once. She was sure Jules meant her when he referred to Rochester's feelings for the recalcitrant Jane. Did it mean he wanted her on a long-term basis? He'd said he had no intention of asking her to marry him, but perhaps, as Sarabeth had thought, that had been protection against her rejection. Bemused by her thoughts, Frankie heard no more of the other poets who read than if they'd been leaves rustling in the wind. She sat in her dark corner, thoughts tumbling in her brain like clothes in a dryer.

People began to rise, and she realized with a start that the meeting was over. Poets and listeners alike headed purposefully for the jugs of wine and apple juice on a side table. Head down, Frankie worked her way toward the door.

She wasn't able to escape. Jules's hand fell on her arm when she was a scant five feet from the door. "Going somewhere?"

Foolishly she stammered, feeling caught. "I—I was just—"

"Fine. I'll join you." He took her arm and walked her briskly to the sidewalk. "Where to?"

Frankie looked both ways. "My car's here somewhere...."

"We won't need it." Still holding her arm, he turned her toward downtown. "We'll go have some coffee or something and you can tell me what you thought of it."

She didn't pretend to misunderstand him. "Jules,

I know nothing about literary matters. You said it yourself. Anything I could tell you would be—would be—''

"Totally without an axe to grind," he interrupted. "Except, of course, for the fact that I was writing about you."

She stopped for a moment, looking up at him earnestly. "No, not just about me. You were talking about yourself too. You were talking about us."

He searched her eyes intently in the dim light, as if he would probe further, but instead took her arm again and set off down the sidewalk. "We can go to that coffeehouse with the bakery, or to a bar. Take your pick."

Relief that he wasn't going to press her warred with irrational disappointment. She made her voice light. "Is there any choice?"

"Right." He grinned down at her. "Bakery it is."

They chose huge gooey chocolatey desserts and coffee and talked comfortably with their elbows on the table, their delight in each other's company a tangible force. They spoke of nothing important or personal, and yet every word, every inflection seemed to Frankie to carry the intimacy of being lovers. Contentment filled her like a flood of warmth and light, especially when he mentioned casually he'd sent Sheila on her way. Frankie scraped the last bit of frosting off her plate and stared longingly at Jules's leftovers.

Laughing, he traded plates with her. "Where do you put all that?" he teased, pinching her upper arm gently. "I don't recall seeing a single spot on your body that could accommodate two pieces of chocolate cake."

His eyes were warm and caressing, and she could feel the fire creeping up her cheeks. "I could eat half a cake and never show it," she bragged. "I work it off."

"Oh yeah?" His fingers trailed down her arm and rubbed sensuously along her palm. Her body began to tingle with heat. "Would you like to get a little exercise tonight?"

"What—what do you have in mind?" She licked her lips in unconscious invitation, and let her hand steal under the table to find his knee. His eyes darkened.

"First," he said, his voice a husky whisper, "we go back to your place. Then, we experiment with an exercise routine that I think you'll find—interesting. We may have to practice quite a bit to get it right."

She swallowed. "Sounds quite—strenuous. I like my exercise to be strenuous."

"Oh, it will be." His eyes held smoky promise. "Shall we?"

He hustled her back to her car so fast she was panting when they got there. "Is this what you meant by exercise?" She collapsed into the driver's seat, her chest heaving. "Because if so—"

Jules slid across the seat and pinned her against the window with hungry intent. His lips were hot and urgent on hers, plundering, pleading, making her tremble. "Frankie," he groaned, "can you drive fast?"

She drove as fast as she could. His hands nearly brought her to grief several times in the short journey, as he let them roam wantonly over her. But when they finally made it into her bedroom, shedding their clothes so quickly they seemed to vanish by magic, he slowed the pace. He lingered over every curve and hollow, letting her touch and explore his own contradictory hardness-softness, until they could no longer withstand their trembling, surging needs and their bodies met, over and over, fire igniting fire until only the embers remained.

He caressed her dreamily, his hands light and delicate on her smooth back. "I don't want to go home," he whispered into her hair. "Why don't you offer me something tempting for breakfast so I have to stay?"

"I can't cook," Frankie mumbled, suppressing a mighty yawn. It was so comfortable to have his warm, slighly damp body pressed so close to hers. She pulled the covers up over them both and snuggled closer to him. He turned her so that her back curved into his body, his hands gently cupping her breasts.

"You don't have to cook," he told her just before she drifted off to sleep. "You're a tempting dish in the raw."

SHE WOKE IN THE MORNING to his gentle insistence, the warm languorous desire flooding her before she was fully conscious. They were still clasped, front to back, and he entered her as she yawned and stretched, sending a deliciously abandoned thrill through her body. His hands toyed lazily with her nipples, teasing until they peaked erectly, while the unhurried sweet movement of his hips had her arching in response. She turned her head and their lips met, their tongues slipping busily into each other's mouths, setting off fiery alarms everywhere. Slowly, achingly, they twisted and turned, finding new responses in each minute adjustment. One of his hands slipped from her breast to probe the secrets of the soft down beneath her belly, and suddenly she was exploding, taking him with her in a frenzy of fulfillment.

She drifted into total awareness, vaguely noting how right it felt to wake beside him, how comfortable and warm it seemed. He smoothed her hair back from her forehead and stared into her eyes. "I love waking up with you," he murmured, brushing a kiss across her lips. "You're wonderful, Frankie. We're wonderful together."

She nodded in mute agreement, unable to put into words the feelings that overwhelmed her. They hugged tightly, and then he slapped her naked posterior. "What are you lollygagging in bed for, woman? Where's my vittles?"

She giggled. "In a series of boxes in the cupboard. Let's see, you could have those toasty little O's of oats, or those crispy little puffs of rice, or—"

"Arrgh!" He clutched his throat, letting his eyes bug out. "It's a mystery to me how you stay alive. Tell you what. If you take a shower with me, I'll fix you breakfast."

They lingered in the shower until the hot water became suspiciously lukewarm, and Frankie had a guilty thought of her roommate, who also liked a morning shower. In the kitchen, Jules found some eggs and the last of a piece of ham, and began deftly cooking omelets. Frankie was laughing at him across the table, raising her laden fork to her lips, when she had a sudden chill of déjà vu. She had been sitting there the day before, bewildered and confused, when Sarabeth had found her. She glanced instinctively at the kitchen door, and Sarabeth stood there, her hair a little mussed, looking younger than her usual suave self in her velour robe.

"I thought I heard voices," Sarabeth mumbled

around a yawn. She squinted at Jules. "I *did* hear voices."

"This is Jules Jones," Frankie hastened to say. "My roommate, Sarabeth Connolly."

Jules and Sarabeth greeted each other politely, and Sarabeth excused herself. Frankie listened apprehensively and caught the sound of a muttered curse from the bathroom as the water turned on. "Maybe we should get going," she suggested to Jules. "Breakfast was great, thanks."

"I liked the appetizer best." He pulled her out of her chair and held her close for a moment. "Good grief, woman, I can't keep my hands off you."

"Vice versa," she muttered, letting her palms slide beneath the Charlotte Bronte T-shirt. Their kisses grew more feverish. She lost herself in the exploration of his scent, finding different tastes and textures all over his neck, discovering again the sensitive hollow of his throat. He was making lazy circles up and down her back while nibbling gently on her earlobe. Sarabeth had to cough twice before they noticed her.

"I think you two could use a little of what I just had," she said sweetly, brushing past them through the doorway and heading for the refrigerator. "A cold shower," she added, glancing meaningfully at Frankie.

"Uh, we have to go to work now. Bye, Sarabeth." Frankie seized Jules and pulled him out to her car.

"Wait! I thought we were going to take another shower."

"The water's cold, you ninny." She hopped in the car and started it, barely waiting for him to shut his door before she was gunning down the driveway.

"Nothing's cold when I'm around you," he said.

It should have sounded corny, like a come-on, but the sincerity of his voice shook her. She looked at him and nearly ran over her neighbor's cat.

They parted at the parking lot of the community college where he'd left his car overnight. When she was alone, Frankie's mood altered slightly. Again she conjured up the confusion she'd felt the day before, compared with this day. She was still confused, she knew, but underneath it all was the feeling that things were going to be all right—more than all right. For the first time in her entire life, things were going to be very, very fine.

She stopped in at her office before going on to the tank, wanting to get some red pens out of the desk. Beatrix Jones was sitting in a chair in front of the window, tapping cigarette ash nervously into the wastebasket.

She greeted Frankie irritably. "Well, you certainly keep bankers' hours here, Miss Warburton. It's past nine o'clock. Does my husband know what time you deign to come in to work?"

Frankie summoned her poise. "I doubt he cares to concern himself with such mundane details, Mrs. Jones." She got the red pens out of her drawer and hesitated, clutching them. "Did you want to see me?"

Trix got up, stubbing her toe slightly on the wastebasket in the process. She glared at Frankie. "I wouldn't be here if I didn't want to see you. I'm not in the habit of sitting in strange offices for no reason at all."

Frankie perched on the edge of her desk. "I don't mind a little chat," she said mildly, "but if you want to be insulting, you'll have to talk to yourself. I do have work to do."

Trix made a visible effort to control herself and

sat down again. She was silent for a moment, and Frankie had almost decided to walk out when Trix began to speak. "I will probably make a mess of this," the older woman muttered. "But I felt I had to come." She took a deep breath. "I can tell you're in love with my son, Miss Warburton." She held up her hand to forestall Frankie's comments. "Please don't interrupt me. What's more, I can tell my son's in love with you." She sighed. "I simply want to tell you that I do not...oppose your marrying him."

Frankie sat very still. Whatever she had expected, it wasn't this. "What—how come?" She stumbled awkwardly over the words.

Trix sighed again as she stubbed out her cigarette. "I had made other plans for Jules." She glanced sharply at Frankie. "Perhaps you noticed that Sheila Madison is—that I was—"

"I noticed," Frankie said gently.

"I thought she would be a good wife for him. Would give him an edge over Grif when it comes to the crunch for the presidency. A corporate president must be capable of entertaining the right people in the right way." Trix was speaking almost to herself, clenching her hands in the lapels of her lush mink coat. "But—well, I've been thinking about it since that dinner you were at. Jules is obviously besotted by you—I've never seen him act this way before." There was resentment in her voice. "If he feels that way about you, there's no use thinking that he'd marry to please me. He's never done anything else to please me."

Trix lit another cigarette and tossed the match irritably toward the wastebasket. It fell on the floor. "I just wanted to tell you privately," she continued when Frankie didn't speak. "I wanted to say that I know we got off on the wrong foot. I'm willing to do what I can to make you feel like part of the family."

The speech was stilted and cold, yet Frankie could recognize the enormous effort that it must have cost the woman to make it. She was touched and impressed. "I—I admire you for being so—magnanimous," she said, trying not to sound sarcastic. "But you're a little ahead of yourself here, Mrs. Jones. Jules hasn't asked me to marry him."

Trix closed her eyes hopelessly. "Great. My son plans to live in sin in front of the whole world. Just what I needed to hear."

"There's nothing like that in the works either," Frankie assured her, feeling an hysterical urge to laugh wildly.

Trix stubbed out her cigarette. "Don't try to fool me," she said darkly. "Jules will ask you to marry him sooner or later. And you'd be a fool not to. My son is quite a catch for anyone."

For a moment this tactless speech set Frankie's back up. But it was the truth, after all, especially as Trix saw it. "You're right about that," she agreed guilelessly.

Trix unbent a little. "I've always wanted to be closer to Jules—and Irene," she said wistfully. "But I simply don't get along well with children, and before I knew it they weren't children anymore. And they were always rebelling, always despising me and my family, my values...." She looked down at her hands, smoothing the mink of her jacket absently. "I suppose Jules has told you about Irene."

Frankie nodded. "A little."

Trix looked up, and Frankie realized with a shock that there were tears shining in her eyes.

"She has a little girl, my granddaughter, and I've never even seen her. Irene has never invited me to visit, even when the baby came. I sometimes wonder why anyone has children. They hurt you so much!"

Frankie was overcome with a rush of sympathy. She wanted to go to Trix, give her a hug, provide some of the human warmth that mink was no match for. But she sensed that Jules's mother had been out of touch with her feelings for some time, and would resent any overtures from someone she regarded as a virtual stranger. Instead, Frankie tactfully handed her a box of tissues and turned away.

"You know," she said conversationally when the sound of nose blowing had ceased, "I'll bet Irene doesn't realize you're waiting for an invitation. I'll bet she feels hurt that her mother has never come out to visit, not even when the baby was born."

There was silence behind her for a moment. She turned. Trix's face wore a faraway, considering look. Then she caught Frankie's eyes on her and straightened her shoulders.

"All this is wandering from the point," she snapped. "I have a great deal of work to do this afternoon, Miss Warburton. My service club has a goal of raising three hundred thousand dollars for the refugee children, and it's my responsibility to coordinate that." She checked the jeweled watch on one wrist and rose to her feet. "I have a meeting to attend. I think we understand one another."

Frankie smiled. "I think we do. And please, call me Frankie. Whether we're to be part of the same family or not, I'm glad you came today." She looked around for her handbag. "Can I help you toward your goal with a contribution for the children?"

Trix left a few moments later, tucking Frankie's generous check into her handbag. She paused and squeezed Frankie's hand briefly. "I—appreciate what you said—about Irene. You may be right." She dropped Frankie's hand and fastened her jacket. "Thank you for the donation, Frankie. I look forward to seeing you again."

The surprising thing, Frankie thought as she dropped back into her desk chair, was that Trix meant it. And she herself wouldn't mind seeing Jules's mother again. The woman definitely had more on the ball than she had realized.

She reached for the listings and went over them for a diligent hour, but her mind kept wandering and finally she let it go. She put her feet on her desk and began to review her entire acquaintance with Julian Jones, from the moment she'd approached him in the parking lot to the moment they'd parted that morning. A pattern began to emerge.

They shared a deep physical attraction. A smile tugged at her lips when she thought of the marvel of their lovemaking. Before Jules, she had never thought there was a sensation as powerful as she found lying in his arms.

But there was more than that. They never ran out of things to say to each other. They argued, certainly. She decided that she liked this. There was a tang to disagreement when you could trust the other person to listen to you, to respect your viewpoint, but to assert his own beliefs as rigorously as you asserted yours.

He could be infuriating. But she couldn't get too worked up about it. When she tried to focus on his faults, his tendency to believe he was always right—when she *knew* she was always right—his ability to switch his attention from the abstract to the concrete without having to change gears, the faults began to assume the characteristics of virtues.

He was sometimes overbearing, sometimes impatient. But everything about him was rapidly assuming a rosy glow. She ached to see him again, she trembled at the thought of kissing him. But the physical sensations were being overwhelmed by something powerful that wanted to have him across from her at the breakfast table for the rest of her life, to work in the garden together, to talk and laugh and share all the important things life could hold.

"We could have our terminals side by side," she murmured dreamily. "We could share a printer." She thought for a moment. "No, I think I want my own printer." She shook her head and tried to return to her work, but without success. "I'm goofy over the guy," she said, staring at the toes of her loafers. "I'm in love with him."

The moment she said the words they felt right. She had been in love with him all along, probably. For years she had been protecting herself unknowingly against any man's desertion because her father had let her grow up alone. Now she was stripped of her defense, naked and soft. But before she could be afraid she thought of Jules. She could trust him. He would stay.

She wanted to run to him, tell him of her discovery, blurt out her love. But some deep feminine impulse made her hold back. There were conventions for this sort of thing. She dismissed the convention that would have her wait for Jules's declaration before she made her own. He had the right to hear it from her, and she wouldn't deny him. But the trappings—the candlelight, the intimate setting—were important and she wanted to savor the experience.

She spent half an hour trying to compose a suitable invitation to dinner—seductive without being coy—and finally gave up in disgust. After phoning the fabricators, and finding out it would be another day before the board was finished, she threw her listings into her car and drove home.

Sarabeth was doing some contract programming for a small computer company on her home terminal, but she came to the door of the workroom when she heard Frankie walk down the hall. "I thought you'd be working at Jones Morton today."

Frankie put the pile of listings on her table and faced Sarabeth. "I'm in love with the guy."

Sarabeth raised an eyebrow. "So what else is new?"

"Why didn't you tell me how great love is?" Frankie twirled around and nearly tripped over a chair. Rubbing her shin absentmindedly, she grinned at Sarabeth. "It's great stuff."

"You've got it bad, hmm?"

"A lifelong case." Frankie sat in the chair, spinning it till she felt dizzy. "I thought I might invite him over to dinner one of these nights and ask him to marry me," she added offhandedly.

"Oh, indeed." Sarabeth shook her head in tolerant disbelief. "We're so casual about it all, we with the cold-blooded logical approach to life."

Frankie felt drunk with love. It was powerful to admit it, to throw in her lot with all the others through the ages who had been willing to risk their emotional lives for the heady feeling of love. "Logical shmogical," she said airily. "Don't speak of the past. I'm a different woman now. Why, I haven't even—"

She stopped abruptly, the words piling up behind her lips. Sarabeth, involved with her program, asked casually over her shoulder, "Haven't what?" When Frankie didn't answer, she turned. "Frankie, you're white as a sheet! What's the matter?"

Frankie made her numb lips move. "I—I haven't even been using birth control," she whispered, her voice shaking. "I just realized it. I must have been—must have been crazy! What—what—"

Sarabeth came over and slipped a comforting arm around her. "Hey, don't panic. Chances are good you've got nothing to worry about. Are you late or anything?"

Frankie shook her head and forgot to stop shaking it. "I won't know...for a few more days." Impatiently she pushed Sarabeth away. "Don't be nice to me. I deserve to be scolded for being so irresponsible!" She jumped to her feet and paced the small dimensions of the room. "I don't know what got into me."

"Honey, don't make a federal case of it." Sarabeth met Frankie's glare innocently. "So you accidentally-on-purpose forgot to take precautions. Kicking yourself now isn't going to help any."

"On purpose!" Frankie collapsed against her desk. "You think I did it on purpose? Subconsciously or something? I guess you're right." She began to gnaw on her fingernail. "What will I do? What if I'm pregnant?" There was a small mirror on the wall near Sarabeth's terminal. She ran to it anxiously and examined her face. "Are there any early symptoms? Is there any way to tell now?"

Sarabeth picked up a nail file. "I've heard that your neck swells," she offered coolly. "Have you noticed your shirt feeling tighter lately?"

Frankie looked at her disgustedly. "You're a lot of help, Sarabeth. Where's your womanly solidarity?"

"I'm saving it for when you really need it." Sarabeth pointed the nail file at Frankie. "Rational thinking is supposed to be your forte, Ms Warburton. Pull yourself together and apply yourself to the problem. Either you're pregnant, or you're not. If you are, you can have the baby or not have it. If you're not, you presumably have nothing to worry about. Now you take it from there."

Thus abjured, Frankie got a grip on herself. "You're right," she agreed, sitting down on the edge of the desk again. "I simply have to consider my options. But there aren't very many, because I won't have an abortion." She answered Sarabeth's raised eyebrows with a decided nod. "I could never do that to Jules's baby. No, if I'm pregnant, I'll be a mother nine months from now." She regarded her roommate with gloomy eyes. "I'll have to go away. If I tell Jules I'm pregnant, he'll feel obliged to marry me. I couldn't face that. I'll go away and bear my child alone."

"Pretty melodramatic," was Sarabeth's comment. "It *is* Jules's baby too. Doesn't he have the right to be with his child?"

Frankie thought furiously. "I'll have to tell him," she concurred. "If he wants, we'll share the child. Six months with me, six with Jules."

Sarabeth put away her nail file. "Does this mean you're not going to ask Jules to marry you?"

"How can I now?" Frankie was too restless to sit. She got up to pace once again. "I can't pressure him like that. And his mother—everyone will think I tried to trap him." She remembered Gamma's pungent comments on the reason for Jules's parents' marriage. Would history repeat itself? "Marriage is out of the question."

Stretching her arms above her head, Sarabeth swiveled in her chair to turn off her computer. "Well, this is as interesting as any hypothetical discussion, I suppose." She sauntered over to the door. "But I have to get ready. Roger will be here in half an hour."

Momentarily distracted from her own problems, Frankie looked up. "Roger? What happened to Desmond?"

Sarabeth shrugged. "I won't be seeing Desmond anymore." A hint of steel crept into her voice. "I went over to his place the other night to surprise him with an intimate little dinner—the sort of thing you were going to do for Jules. He's been working late a lot, with no time for going out—or so he told me. I found him and his secretary getting a little extracurricular work in on the side." She shrugged disdainfully. "Imagine—I was thinking a lot about what I told you—about risking everything for love, about the pain being worth it if the love is worth it. I even thought Desmond might be The One. Was I ever wrong!" She looked at Frankie's stricken face. "Oh, now, honey, I shouldn't have told you that. Don't you worry. Just because I got shot down doesn't mean you will too. I've never been lucky at love. I think you will be."

Frankie stared blankly at the door after Sarabeth left. Were the lovely, rosy feelings she'd been having only an illusion after all? She seemed to hear the crashing sounds of her brave new world as it tumbled around her ears. Maybe she was having a breakdown. Her chest felt tight, and there was a ringing sound in her ears that wouldn't go away, though she shook her head impatiently. Then came Sarabeth's voice.

"Phone for you, Frankie." Her footsteps came down the hall outside the workroom door, and she stuck her head around the doorjamb. "It's Jules."

10

JULES'S VOICE was relaxed, expansive. "Listen. I got to thinking about your illiterate approach to poetry, and I decided to educate you a little. I'll bring the verse, you provide the food. Tonight, your place. Okay?"

Here he was, suggesting the sort of evening she'd had in mind when she'd bounced home that afternoon. Candlelight, the two of them picnicking on the floor in front of the fireplace, he reading some exquisite love poem—the perfect setting for her proposal of marriage. Now, saddled with the burden of her irresponsible behavior, Frankie felt paralyzed with fear.

"Well, what do you say?" She tried to force speech past her dry lips. "Frankie, are you there?"

"Arh," she croaked. "Uh, Jules—"

"Great. I'll see you around six-thirty." He hung up.

She stared blankly at the receiver. He hadn't given her a chance to suggest that they not see each other for a few days. Now she would have to meet him with all the uncertainty of her possible pregnancy hanging over her.

"I'm not pregnant," she said firmly, trying to take control of her life. But there was no way to deny the risk she'd taken—and for what reason? It was so foreign to her nature to be careless in matters that were important.

Well, there was no point in borrowing trouble, as
Sarabeth had tried to tell her. She would meet things
as they came, instead of anticipating problems
where none might exist. She strode purposefully to
the kitchen and pulled open the refrigerator door.
The interior was not promising. A carton of milk, a
rind of moldy cheese, two shriveled hot dogs, a tub
of margarine and a couple of soft drinks were all
that she saw. She opened the vegetable keeper.
Three limp carrots and an unidentified grayish-
blackish mass stared back at her. She shut the
vegetable keeper hastily.

Sarabeth came in, fastening her earrings. "Why
don't we have any food around here?" Frankie
said pettishly. "We eat, don't we? Where does it
come from?"

"*I* eat," Sarabeth corrected her. "But I go out to
do it. You, on the other hand, simply consume
enough calories to keep you on your feet. If I recall
correctly, the last time you went to the grocery
store was to get a good deal on a case of Ding-
dongs."

Frankie sat limply at the table. "You're right. I
always thought the Colonel knew more about
cooking than I did, so I let him do it. But there's
Jules coming over to read poetry to me—I can't
serve him a basket of takeout chicken! What'll I
do?"

Sarabeth walked over and looked at the contents
of the refrigerator judicially. "Beef Wellington is
obviously out." She took pity on Frankie's woebe-
gone expression. "There's a fancy deli in that market near El Camino. They have more variety than
the Colonel. Just go pick out the most romantic-
looking things and you'll be fine."

Frankie actually enjoyed herself in the deli. She

chose marinated mushrooms, some grape leaf-wrapped rice appetizers, a couple of soft ripe cheeses and the appropriate crackers to eat them on, and freshly made ravioli in a cream sauce, that the clerk assured her needed only to be heated up. Getting into the spirit of the evening, she disregarded the aisle of Twinkies and Sno-balls and headed for the classy bakery she'd heard the secretaries at Jones Morton talking about. She found chocolate cheesecake, eclairs and little tarts, which she bought with abandon. By the time she got her booty home, it was 6:15.

She rushed into a clean T-shirt and threw a couple of logs into the fireplace. The May evening wasn't really cold, but a fire was not totally unwarranted. Rummaging in the dining room's corner cupboard, she found a lace tablecloth sent to her long ago by an aunt who had a misguided impression of her niece's way of entertaining. But tonight the tablecloth would come in handy. She spread it carefully in front of the fireplace and stood back for a moment.

Seizing her scissors, she ran outside and gleaned the choicest blooms from her roses and carnations. She stuck them hastily into an old bean crock and was charmed with their unexpected air of jauntiness. Using the china and silver Sarabeth had inherited from her grandmother, Frankie set two places at her improvised table. At 6:29 she was rummaging frantically in the corner cupboard for candles. At 6:31, when Jules rang the doorbell, her setting was complete with the soft light of the only candle she'd been able to find, a huge globe that supposedly depicted the planet Jupiter and its moons.

Jules had one arm full of books, but he used the

other one to gather her close. "Mmm," he breathed, nibbling delicately at her lips. "You taste delicious."

"Don't spoil your appetite," she whispered back, falling under the spell of his nearness. For a moment, as their lips tasted each other with tiny teasing kisses, she was able to forget her difficulties. But when he pushed her inside and dropped his books on the floor to draw her closer, memory came flooding back.

"I—I have to finish a couple of things in the kitchen." She looked up at him and nearly forgot to move. When she saw him through the eyes of love, without the denial that had been her constant companion, she could almost swoon from the fullness of emotion that he inspired in her. With a fierce upsurge of primitive feeling she wanted to claim him, brand him as hers, make sure no other woman got near her prize.

She blinked and realized she'd been staring at him. His eyes were amused but a little puzzled. "Do you want some help?" He steered her in the right direction. "I didn't bring any poetry about cooking, but perhaps I could improvise." While she busied herself with careful reheating of the ravioli and set out the rest of the food on a tray, he leaned back in a chair and made up nonsense limericks.

There was a young man—code-named Nemo—
who was crazy about a young femo,
He took her some flowers
and stayed there for hours,
till she asked him to leave with a screamo.

By the time she had the food assembled Frankie was laughing too hard to carry in the tray. Jules did it for her, exclaiming about the feast ahead. He pulled a volume of Keats from his pile of books and read "The Eve of St. Agnes": "These delicates he heaped with glowing hand...." Frankie listened, entranced by the music of the words. Jules read well, his mobile voice expressing the feelings of the lovers, lingering over the voluptuous syllables.

When they had miraculously eaten everything but dessert, Frankie piled the contents of the bakery boxes on one plate and Jules picked up John Donne's poems. "The best poet for lovers," he declared, his eyes hot on her. "Listen:"

License my roving hands, and let them go,
Behind, above, before, between, below,
O my America! my new-found-land....

Her dessert forgotten, she found herself close to Jules, nestled in the warm crook of his arm, while his voice sang enchantments in her ear. Gradually the heat of his thigh against hers kindled a more intimate warmth within her. She stopped listening to the words, hearing only the music, thinking only of the embers that sparked as she pressed against him.

Subtly, sensuously, she began to tease him, moving so that the full globe of her breast strained against his side, her nipple hardening into a nudge of desire. She let her hand rest lightly on his thigh, kneading the muscle with fingers that traveled with sure instinct across the taut denim. Each tiny movement seemed to fan her own arousal to a disproportionate degree.

His voice was starting to thicken. When she turned her head his neck was temptingly close, the pulse throbbing rapidly under the tanned skin. Impulsively she leaned closer and flicked her tongue to taste the leaping pulse. His voice faltered; she felt him shudder. He moved like quicksilver, bearing her down to the thick carpet, pinning her shoulders. She gazed up at him, unblinking. His breath fanned her hair in fast hard pants.

"Woman." His words were husky, slurred. "You play with fire—" His mouth came down and hovered tormentingly over hers. "You're gonna get burned."

The dryness in her mouth seemed transferred to her lips. She licked them, imagining that his heat seared her. "Yes, please," she whispered achingly.

Their clothes seemed to melt away. They made love once in a fast furious rush of passion, next to the remains of dessert and the discarded poetry of John Donne. Afterward, relaxed and contented in the warmth of the fire, Frankie lay drowsily while he busied himself with a pen and a blank sheet of paper, sketching her nude figure with bold seductive sweeps of line. She was fascinated by his skill but, prudishly, worried about the accuracy with which her body had been depicted. "Jules, what if someone finds it?"

Laughing, he threw the sketch on the fire. "I don't need it," he told her when she protested such a rash move. "I have a thousand pictures of you in my mind." His hands moved delicately over her as his eyes drifted shut. "I could draw you blindfolded," he whispered, touching her with gentle fingers that slowly changed from satisfied to hungry. Then he carried her into her room, laying her on the bed as tenderly as any bridegroom, showing her ecstasy that went beyond sensation.

She drifted into sleep in his arms, but she woke knowing it was still evening. Jules was gone; she listened for a startled moment and heard the water running in the kitchen, accompanied by off-key singing. Stretching, she took a caftan off the hook behind her door and padded to the kitchen.

Jules didn't hear her approach. He had cleared away the remains of dinner from in front of the fireplace, and he was washing the dishes with much splashing and the lusty rendition of sea chanties. She watched him for a moment, loving the way his brown hair curled over the collar of his rugby shirt, and the springy, almost cocky way he moved. He turned and saw her.

"I'm sorry, love. I wanted to get back to you before you knew I was gone."

She went over and pushed the hair off his forehead, smoothing it back lovingly. "You're a real sweetie pie, Jones. You didn't have to do this."

He shrugged it off. "Compared to the *Nautilus*'s galley, this kitchen is as roomy as the wide open spaces. Besides, I didn't want the leftovers to spoil." He leered at her wolfishly. "What would I have for breakfast if the cheesecake got rancid overnight?"

Frankie felt the stirrings of hunger. "There was cheesecake left?"

He turned back to the sink. "Most of the munificent desserts you provided didn't get eaten—I don't know why." Frankie opened the refrigerator. It still looked a bit bare, but the bakery boxes made a brave show. She picked one at random and found she had the eclairs.

Jules heard her when she opened the box, though she was trying to be quiet. "Aha! Planning to snarf the eclairs behind my back! You won't get away with it, me proud beauty."

She edged toward the sink. "Stay away from me, Snydely, or these eclairs will be decorating your face."

"You must give them to me," he hissed, twirling an imaginary mustache and crouching in front of the sink. "Why do you defy me?"

She feinted behind him, trying to reach the dish drainer full of clean plates and glasses. "I simply want to eat my eclair in a civilized manner, with a plate and a fork."

"What! My clean dishes? Touch them not, woman, or you'll find yourself in the suds!" He made a spirited defense of the dish drainer, but relented in the end and let her have a plate. They sat at the table, the plate between them, alternately feeding each other bites and rolling their eyes in ecstasy.

"That beats a Ding-dong all hollow," Frankie said, sitting back with a sigh of repletion. She eyed the second eclair wistfully. Jules put the box back in the refrigerator.

"If we eat any more we'll have to get some exercise," he said, pulling her up to her feet. "And frankly, my dear Frankie, I don't know if I'm up for that."

She smiled up at him. "Is that a challenge?"

He groaned and pulled her closer. "No way, baby. I just want to go back to bed and sleep in your arms all night."

Relaxed and safe in his embrace, Frankie nevertheless felt a shiver course down her back at his words. His calling her "baby" had brought back all the doubt and anguish of the afternoon. But now that she was with him, it seemed foolish to worry about his possible rejection. She loved him. He had told her he loved her—not recently, it was true, but she had no reason to believe his feelings had changed. When two people loved each other, things would work out.

Just the same. she knew she wouldn't propose

tonight, or tell him about her lapse. There was no point in saying anything until she knew if she was pregnant or not. And tonight was so special. She didn't want to take a chance on spoiling things.

She helped him finish the dishes and tidy the living room, and then they climbed back into bed, clasping each other warmly, talking in whispers after Sarabeth came in. She told him stories from her childhood, amazed at the font of reminiscence he could tap in her at will. And he told her of his early life, of visits to Gamma, of the seeds of rivalry with Grif. When they finally went to sleep she felt as if she had never known anyone better than she knew Julian Jones.

She opened her eyes to the sunlight the next morning. Jules was on his stomach, his face pressed into the pillow, his hand twined in her hair. She tried to untangle his fist gently, but he sighed and turned his head. "'Busy old fool, unruly sun,'" he murmured.

"Huh?" She pushed the hair away from his face and ran her thumbnail along the scratchy stubble that adorned his chin.

"Some more Donne," he explained sleepily.

Frankie felt silly. "Hey, I know some literary jokes. I remember them from college." She sat up in bed and recited, "'Elizabeth Barrett is Browning, but John is Donne.'"

That woke him up. "Philistine!' He banged her soundly with the pillow, then held her down, tickling unmercifully. "I can see there's a lot of educating to do with you. I'll teach you some respect for literature if it's the last thing I do."

"Stop!" She wriggled vainly, trying to get away, her sides aching from laughing. "You're—you're hurting me," she gasped.

He stopped immediately. "Did I hurt you? Poor, poor baby. I'm sorry, love." He showered kisses down her face and neck, smoothing back her hair, which lay in tangled drifts over the pillows.

"You didn't really," she said ingenuously. "I just said that to get you to stop." She took his face between her hands and spoke without thinking first, without weighing consequences and results. "I love you, Jules."

She had expected—what, she didn't know. Delirious joy? Exhilarated excitement? Whatever she'd expected, she didn't get it. He smiled blandly and said, "I know you do, love."

Frankie lay still and looked up at him, blinking. "Jules, maybe you didn't hear me correctly. I didn't say I like you, or I want you. I said, I *love* you. You know, the big L-O-V-E."

His smile was tender, but not full of the incredulous joy she'd half expected. "I heard you, Frankie darlin'. And I'm glad you finally said it. I've been waiting for you to realize the situation for days now. But I knew you'd figure it out. You're a pretty smart cookie."

She lay still under the covers, but inside she was seething. It was insulting to be calmly told that something she'd had to agonize over, to come to grips with, was nothing much—simply a "situation" she would "figure out." Her blood began to boil.

"Jules," she said, her voice dangerously soft, "I'm not always as smart as I should be. In the matter of birth control, for instance."

He stiffened. "What are you trying to say, Frankie?"

"I—well, I forgot to use birth control the past few days. Silly of me, wasn't it?" Deliberately she made her voice light, watching him from under her lashes.

This time his reaction was more apparent. "Are you saying you're pregnant? That you could be pregnant?" His grip on her shoulders became unbearably forceful. His eyes bored into her, daring her to continue. But she was still indignant at the offhand way he'd received her avowal of love. Hadn't he realized how momentous that was for her? Let him see what it was like to have someone treat an important event as if it were nothing!

"What does it matter?" She squirmed under his hands. "You're really hurting me now, Jules."

His hands fell away. His face was ashen. "I don't believe I'm hearing this. You, the responsible Ms Warburton, telling me it doesn't matter if you're pregnant or not?" He swung his legs over the side of the bed, watching her with narrowed eyes. "Does your attitude indicate you've already decided what to do if you are pregnant?"

Every line of his body expressed distrust. The anger that flooded her was welcome, stiffening, keeping her from disintegrating at the ease with which he could doubt her. "As a matter of fact," she spat, sitting up in the tumbled covers, "I have decided what to do if I'm pregnant. But before I tell you what I've decided, let's hear what you've decided I've decided!"

His lips twitched, but she refused to exchange outrage for humor. He looked at her, sitting there stark naked, her hair streaming like Lady Godiva's over her breasts, and wished with all his heart that this wasn't happening. But when he thought about what she could be contemplating, he hardened his mind. "I can't quite see you letting a child interfere with your well-regulated life," he said slowly. Anguish that had its roots in his childhood rose up, stifling his reason. "Frankie, please don't have an abortion. You can give the child to me, you don't have to worry about it. Just don't—"

He found that his eyes were squeezed shut, perhaps to prevent any tears from creeping through. When he opened them, his heart sank. Frankie's face wore an expression he'd never seen before, one of stern rigid denial.

When she spoke, her voice was like ice. "I can hardly believe I heard you say that, Julian Jones." Each word stung vehemently. "I was a fool to think you were the one who could change my mind about love. I—I was going to ask you to marry me, not too smart a move. If you loved me, how could you think, even for one minute, that I would—would—" She pulled the sheet up to wipe furiously at her face. Pushing him aside, she sprang out of bed. He stood numbly, conscious that he'd made a big mistake, uncertain how to remedy it.

She pulled underclothes out of a drawer and began to dress, as regardless of him as if he'd been no more than shadow. Summoning his wits, he spoke to her back. "Frankie, I didn't mean to insult you. I don't understand why you threw this at me. The way you said it—surely you can see—" He ran his hands through his hair in frustration and took his own clothes off the chair he'd put them over the night before. "What's the use," he muttered wearily. "If you won't see reason...."

Frankie was wavering. She *had* been cavalier in telling him. After all, the whole thing was hypothetical. But his last words hung in the air and fueled her resolve. This was the kind of thing it was important to find out before a woman made a lifelong mistake. Jules didn't trust her. He assumed the worst about her on very little evidence.

She zipped her jeans and beat her hair into submission with a hairbrush. "Don't tell me about reason," she said, fighting to keep from sounding shrill. "Reason would dictate an altogether different course of action than I'm following." She flung her hair back and faced him defiantly. "Reason tells me to get rid of your baby if I'm pregnant," she said baldly. He whitened, but she could not stop. "Then I could do what you assume I will do and take up my nice, regulated life again, with no more men around to mess me up." She gulped back the tears that threatened, brushing away the few that escaped with both her fists. "But for once in my life I'm not going to listen to reason. Not altogether, anyway." Her smile was a very thin affair. "I won't harm my baby," she said, adding almost automatically, "assuming there *is* a baby. But the part about no more men—well that sounds good to me right now. Get the picture?"

She turned, ready to sweep out of the room. Jules found that he'd tangled his hand in her hair just before she went out the door. He turned her to face him, his hands urgent, his actions dictated by something so deep inside him that he had no control over it. "You can't do this to me, Frankie. I don't care what we've said, this is not the way. Frankie, I love you. You love me. Where's the happy-ever-after part?"

She stared at him, willing herself to be cold, rigid, to tune out the anguish that filled his eyes and distorted his face. "There are no fairy tales in real life," she said dully. "Just like there's no love, really. None at all. I always knew it."

His hands dropped and he stepped away. She

watched his expression change, watched the rage begin to build. "So you're going back in there," he snarled. Instinctively she shrank away. "Back into logic land, where everything is neat and tidy and never to be disturbed. You're a fool, Frankie Warburton." His voice was heavy with scorn, but she didn't let it touch her. Nothing would touch her again. "You let this whole thing escalate, get out of hand, just because your head was afraid to lose control. Well, you've won. I'll go. I don't want any part of life in logic land."

He turned to leave, and she watched, paralyzed. But he wasn't finished yet. "Don't try to hide any pregnancy from me. I'll find out, and I'll do my share. But I really doubt you're going to have my baby. Robots can't conceive, can they?"

His footsteps sounded heavy through the house. When the front door slammed behind him, Frankie moved at last. She took a barrette and bound her hair. Then she stripped the sheets from her bed with mechanical movements, fetching clean ones from the linen closet, smoothing the quilt with hands that had begun to shake. She carried the used sheets to the washer and started the water. Finally she went into the kitchen.

Sarabeth was there, busying herself with the coffee maker. She thrust a cup of coffee into Frankie's numb hands. "I couldn't help but hear," she said, sympathy apparent in her eyes and voice. "Honey child, I'm so sorry. You don't have to talk about it, but I'm here for you."

Frankie gulped some of the coffee, scalding her tongue. The small pain intruded on her deafened senses. Suddenly she could feel again. The tears she'd dammed up broke through her control and flooded down her face. She laid her head on the table and sobbed gustily.

Sarabeth made soothing noises and patted her back, bringing a box of tissues. At last Frankie stopped the flood, blowing her nose and drinking the rest of the coffee. She could feel Sarabeth waiting. "It was...so stupid," she said, hiccuping a little. "It just blew up out of nowhere." She looked at her roommate dolefully.

"He'll be back." Sarabeth sounded confident, but Frankie shook her head.

"No." She thought back over the quarrel. "I don't think so. We both said some unforgivable things. And I think—I think it was really my fault to begin with." She looked at her hands, clenching the fingers to keep from shaking. "Besides," she added, low voiced, "I don't know if I want him back. This hurts too much. If it ever happened again...I couldn't bear it."

Sarabeth shook her head and refilled the coffee cups. "You can bear it," she said softly. "You can bear much more than this, sweetie. Women always have, and they always will." In her eyes Frankie saw the knowledge of her pain reflected. She had time to give Sarabeth a quick, hard hug before she had to run and shut herself in her room and let the misery take her.

11

FRANKIE STOOD IN THE SHADOWS outside the community college and watched the congregation of poets milling around. The late-June dusk was not yet deep enough to hide her successfully. She felt exposed, and willed her feet to go on, past the building and back home. Instead, she found herself inching around laughing groups of people and into the room where she'd sat a few short weeks ago and heard Jules read a poem that had opened her eyes to her love for him.

Even as she found a seat in the back row she castigated herself for the weakness of hoping to see him again. He'd made it clear that he didn't care if he never saw her anymore. She'd picked up her equipment at Jones Morton and finished the prototype work at home, without hearing a single protest from the man who'd been so insistent that she work with him every minute. Now the prototype was done, except for some final programming to do in the next couple of days. After that, there would be no more contact with Julian Jones.

She had received an occasional message from him through the mainframe computer at Jones Morton. The messages had been curt, with no softness about them. She'd had a couple of notes from Gamma, who was distressed that Jules was upset. She'd never answered them. And she'd had constant dreams about Jules, about making love with him, about trying to follow him through a sterile electronic maze. She did her best to bury the dreams every morning.

Now she crouched in her folding chair and wished that the large fellow who'd concealed her at the last meeting would be so obliging again. But the chairs in front of her were occupied by two short, frail-looking elderly ladies, whose blue-veined hands held identical leather-covered portfolios. They put their heads together for a low-voiced gossip, leaving Frankie feeling as if she towered behind them like a two-headed giant.

She sat miserably through the first poems, wishing she'd never come, wishing she had the nerve to leave. But she'd spotted Jules, sitting near the front, the same nervous, quick-talking woman beside him with her hand almost constantly on his arm. Frankie was torn between the desire not to take her eyes off Jules and the fear that he would somehow be able to feel her watching him, that he would turn and see her and she would see his face freeze again as it had just before he'd left her standing in her bedroom. The back of his head was as familiar to her as her own backyard. She looked at the crisp curls that came just to the neck of his T-shirt, and let herself imagine that she was running her fingers through his hair, that they were together once again. Then, ashamed, she caught herself up. Realizing that she clutched the metal edge of her chair until it bit into her hands, she forced herself to relax.

Jules's name was called, the sound of it like an embodiment of her fantasies. She jumped involuntarily, her hands closing again around the chair edge. The two old ladies in front of her put their white heads together as Jules took his place at the podium. Their voices twittered in her ears while her eyes devoured his face. "So pale—" the old ladies were saying to each other. Jules must be a favorite of theirs. "Positively ill—"

He was pale. His eyes looked huge, burning behind the horn-rims. His hair was longer than she remembered, and with a slight shock she realized that it had been nearly four weeks since she'd seen him. He was wearing the Shakespeare T-shirt again, and it evoked vivid memories of him standing in the sunshine by her car, the first time they'd met. Even then he'd had an effect on her she hadn't been able to explain. How could she live without him?

His eyes roamed the crowd and found her as if she'd been the only one in the audience. The light caught his horn-rims, hiding his expression, but she saw the muscles by his mouth tighten. He had been holding a notebook but he put it down, his hands closing on each side of the podium as if it were holding him up.

She didn't expect his voice to sound so normal. "I decided to read something different, if you don't mind, Maggie," he said, nodding toward the woman who'd served as moderator. "It's a ballad." He cleared his throat. "A rewrite of 'Frankie and Johnny'; I'm sure you're all familiar with that."

Frankie's heart stopped beating. His voice rang out, louder than the night he'd opened her ears to poetry, the liquid, melodious effect submerged harshly.

Frankie and Johnny were lovers—
they thought what they felt was above
everything else! They pledged to be true,
but you know how that goes in love.
She was his woman, but she didn't stay long.

His voice went on and on, pouring out a bitter story of betrayal that found an answering chord in the audience. They responded to the evident emotion in his words. When at last he was quiet the room rocked with applause.

Frankie barely heard it. She felt every word like a spear aimed directly at her. The fragile shell she was trying to maintain between herself and the world was no defense. She had to leave. Stumbling over the knees and feet of the others in her row, she looked wildly for any door but the front door—the one by which the podium stood. There was a door in the opposite corner. She wrenched it open and found a classroom full of people beyond it. Uncaring, she fled through the room toward the outside door.

"Miss, are you all right?" The instructor, a young man with a pointer who stood by a blackboard full of incomprehensible foreign phrases, took a couple of hesitant steps toward her. But Frankie shook her head and dashed out the door, determined to put as much space as possible between herself and the scene of so much agonized humiliation.

Jules was waiting right outside in the hallway. She ran full tilt into his arms, looked at him in horror and wrenched herself away. Rubbing the tears out of her eyes with her sleeve, she stumbled through the entrance of the community college and into the welcome dark anonymity of the street. When she heard his footsteps behind her she started running again.

He caught her before she reached the corner, whirling her to face him. "Can't take it? What's the matter? Is the human side trying to break out again?" His voice cut at her. His eyes were implacable behind the lenses.

"Don't!" She tried to pull her arm away. "Don't—" Then he was holding her, crushing her against his chest. She felt exquisite pain run along every point of contact between their bodies. "Don't take it all away!" she pleaded, weeping, not knowing what she said.

"All what?" Jules held her head tightly against his chest, afraid to look at her, afraid one glance would betray him. What a fool he'd been to search for her face in the audience, to come after her when she'd left the reading. But the distress on her face smote him. *She deserves it*, he told himself fiercely. *She deserves the same kind of hell I've been living in.* When he felt her shaking, tenderness stirred within him. *Fool*, he raged at himself. *Fool!* But still he held her, his hands unconsciously gentling.

She felt the change and froze, her heart seizing any excuse, no matter how frail, to hope. She pulled away, not wanting to throw her love on the ground for him to finish flattening.

"Take all what away?" His voice was low.

She had control of herself at the moment. She would not break down again. "Nothing. It doesn't matter." She took a deep breath. "You could at least have changed my name."

He shrugged, his face taking on an ironic smile. "It was just an old ballad, brought up to date. The names were a coincidence."

"Sure." She mimicked his smile and turned away. "Be seeing you, Jones. Good luck on your project."

His hand shot out and caught her arm. "Wait a minute, Ms Warburton. How's our baby?"

She kept her eyes fixed on the pavement. Her voice was dull. "There is no baby. I wasn't pregnant." That gave away nothing of her feelings when her period had started three days after the Big Fight, as Sarabeth called it. As if to underscore her emotional pain, cramps had plagued her, making the week seem endless. Afterward, she'd felt empty, barren, and that had surprised her, because she had expected to feel relieved.

His eyes searched her, hard as obsidian. "So you say. How do I know you're telling the truth?"

She stiffened and pried his fingers from around her arm. "The same way you know anyone is telling the truth. You don't." She glared up at him. "You'll just have to take my word for it." A burst of hysterical laughter escaped her. "God, I'm glad I came tonight after all. I was in danger of forgetting what's so objectionable about you."

Jules watched her hurrying away and cursed his clumsy tongue. "Frankie!" Though he didn't shout, she heard him anyway. He saw her slow down. Breaking into a lope, he caught up with her and shoved his hands into his pockets to help resist the unbearble urge to touch her. "I didn't mean that," he said gruffly. "Of course I trust you, or I wouldn't have let you finish my prototype." He hesitated. "Damn, I don't want thngs to be like this between us!"

Frankie felt the flicker of hope again. This time she didn't squash it down quite so firmly. They stood for a moment on the corner, facing each other awkwardly, neither of them certain what to do next.

Finally Jules said, "I—I'll call you tomorrow. Okay?"

Frankie felt a smile blossom on her face. "Fine. Fine. I'll talk to you then."

He turned back to the community college and she walked swiftly away, the seed of hope sprouting inside her and growing at an alarming rate. She felt light and invincible, as if her feet were a few millimeters off the ground.

It was a ten-minute walk to get home, and toward the end of it she began to caution herself. After all, if there had been a reason for the Big Fight, there was probably a reason not to get back with Jules again. But the cold, cautious part of her had been permanently subdued by the preceding four weeks. If living with only reason and logic as companions was going to be that painful, then she preferred an alternative.

Now wait a moment, her inner voice said. *You don't know what he has in mind yet.* But she could guess. And she didn't want to go back to her neat, self-contained, sterile life. She wanted the risk of love, of really caring for someone else, of feeling loved in return. "If that's not what he wants," she said firmly out loud, getting a curious look from some of the people on the street, "I'll just change his mind for him."

"Sure, lady," said a man. She gave him a brilliant smile and floated by. With each step her confidence grew that she and Jules could resolve their problems. She was tempted to turn and go back to the poetry reading, but some feminine wisdom stopped her. In the morning they would both have had time to think.

She breezed into her house, hungry for the first time in weeks. Sarabeth was in the kitchen, fixing a cup of herb tea. She looked at Frankie with a question on her face.

"I'm starved!" Frankie seized the refrigerator door with enthusiasm. "What do we have to eat?"

"Not much." Sarabeth fished her tea bag out of the cup. "I'm dieting, and you haven't been interested in going to the grocery store lately." She scrutinized Frankie and began to smile. "So, you saw Jules."

"Is it that obvious?"

"Written all over your face."

Embarrassed, Frankie hid her revealing countenance in the refrigerator. "My soul, the cupboard is really bare! What's this?" she brought out a tightly-lidded plastic container.

"Don't open that!" Sarabeth shrieked, but it was too late. Frankie stared at the contents for a horrified moment before she put the lid back on hastily.

"What was it?" she asked finally, her voice hushed.

Sarabeth laughed. "Three-week-old salmon mousse that I brought home in a doggy bag from that fancy new restaurant Charles took me to. I forgot about it for a while, and then I just didn't want to remember it."

Frankie hefted the container, weighing its value as a good leftovers holder, then threw the whole thing into the trash. "Forget it," she said expansively. "Nobody should have to clean out a container with three-week-old salmon mousse in it when I'm so happy."

Sarabeth wiped imaginary sweat from her brow. "Whew! What a relief. It was beginning to haunt my dreams."

"Wait a minute!" Frankie slapped a hand to her forehead. "Charles? What happened to Roger?"

"You have been going around in a daze." Sarabeth stirred honey into her tea and blew on the steamy brew. "Roger is old news. He was boring. Now Charles...." Her face took on a dreamy expression. "Charles is definitely not boring. Definitely."

Frankie found some peanut butter in the cupboard and made herself a sandwich. It was nice that Sarabeth was happy too. Everyone should be happy. Devouring her sandwich, Frankie promised herself a trip to the grocery store the next day. Maybe she would get a cookbook too, and really put her mind to it. After all, cooking couldn't be any more difficult than Fourier transforms.

She filled the watering can and wandered around the house, tending her plants with an absent air. In the workroom she paused to pick up a new listing of the program she was working on for the prototype and leaf through it. It wasn't poetry, but it was elegantly done.

"All meat, no fat," she muttered, flicking through the pages. Here was that place she wasn't too sure about. She sat down at her terminal and dialed the mainframe at Jones Morton. When the computer came up on her terminal screen, she noticed Jules's name in the list of people currently using the system. He must be at his office, since he didn't have a terminal on the *Nautilus*. She was tempted to send him a message—something silly and giggly, something high schoolish—but resisted the temptation.

For a couple of hours she worked steadily, writing code and working back through it to see if it hung together. Finally she finished, leaning back in her chair and stretching her arms above her head. She asked for the list of users, and noticed that only she and Jules were left on the system. Now she couldn't resist. She was composing her message when the screen went blank.

He's beat me to it, she thought. But the message that filled her screen was no lighthearted quip from a lover. "HELPHELPHELP." She stared at the word as it multiplied on her screen. He was sending the message continuously. Even as her brain began to assimilate what it had seen the screen once again went blank.

She typed a frantic message to Jules and got no response. The telephone! She would call Jones Morton and the guard would put her through to Jules and she would find out if this was someone's idea of a joke. The kitchen telephone was a separate line from the one in the workroom, just for occasions when she was using the telephone to tie into someone's mainframe. She rushed to the kitchen phone and punched out the number, her hand trembling so that she could hardly hold the receiver. It rang several times without being answered. She was too impatient to wait. In five minutes she could be at the building, finding out for herself.

The streets were deserted this late in the evening. She all but ignored the stop signs, fretting impatiently when a red light held her immobile for a minute. When she reached the side door where the guard was supposed to check badges of those working late in the building, there was no guard present. She had a key that would unlock the outer door. She went through the small vestibule, past the vacant guard's station, and pushed on the inner door. To her surprise, it opened.

The hall was creepy in the shadowy light, with her footfalls sounding harshly in the empty space. Instinctively she hushed her steps, trying to go as silently as possible. Here was Jules's office—there was his inner door—

The light was on, but the room was empty. The oversized envelope that had held the prototype drawings leaned against the desk, also empty. If Jules had the drawings...she was on her way to the tank before her conscious mind caught up with her fears. The tank was supposed to be a tamper-proof environment. But if technology taught you anything, it was that nothing is resistant to a newer technology.

She moved quietly down the hall again, feeling in her bag for the badge-key that would open the tank door. She'd meant to turn it in the other day when she came by for some listings, but had forgotten. Now she blessed her absentmindedness.

Her fingers found the badge at the bottom of her bag and clutched the hard plastic, feeling a sense of urgency mount inside her. Where was Jules? What if he was at home right at the moment on his houseboat? But in that case, who had sent the "HELP" message? She shook her head and broke into a half lope.

She was almost at the tank door when she ran into a guard. It was the grizzled, older man who had occasionally checked her in when she'd been working evenings. He regarded her suspiciously. "Kind of late to be running around in the halls, Miss."

She clutched his arm, absurdly relieved. "Why weren't you on the door? Where's Jules—Dr. Jones? Have you seen him tonight?"

He scratched his head. "Young Williams is on the side door tonight. And yes, I seen Mr. Jones a couple of hours back, going into the tank there." He jerked his head toward the tank door down the hall. "What's this about the door?"

Briefly Frankie explained that she'd walked in unchallenged, and her reason for being there. The guard was bewildered by her rapid-fire explanation but allowed himself to be dragged to the tank door. Just in case there was trouble, Frankie didn't want to be alone.

She stuck her badge in the door slot and punched in the combination on the keypad, praying that the access code had not been changed in the past few weeks. The door clicked, and she pushed it open, pulling the guard, whose badge bore the name Gordon Rossiter, in after her.

All the lights were on in the tank. Somehow the bright illumination made the windowless room more sinister than shadows would have. Unerringly Frankie headed for a small walled-off area where Jules had established his prototype work. Even in the security of the tank, he'd wanted a locked door between his project and everyone else's.

The lights were on behind the clouded-glass partition, but there was no answer to Frankie's tentative "Jules?" She called again, trying the door handle. It turned easily under her fingers. She pushed it open, the guard behind her.

Inside was chaos. The prototype board was a mangled piece of electronic meat, its integrated circuits sprouting wildly from the twisted printed circuit board like severed fingers. The drawings were strewn over the space, large black blotches of ink still glistening on their mutilated surfaces. The acrid smell of smoked circuitry hung in the air above the smashed chassis of microprocessors. One of the terminals dangled from the desk by its keyboard connector cord, while the other terminal belched its innards from a gaping hole in the screen.

In the middle of the carnage was Jules, sprawled over the desk, the keyboard beneath him. A slow river of red ran down the side of the desk and dripped on the floor.

Frankie never knew how she got through the

chaos of equipment to his side. She reached a trembling hand to his head. He was warm, and under her fingers he shifted and groaned. She sagged with relief.

The guard still stood in the doorway. "Lawks a mercy," he said finally. "Somebody's been busy in here."

Frankie felt for Jules's pulse. It was faint and rapid, and the blood gushed from an ugly wound on the back of his head when she tried to move him. She looked around wildly for something to stem the flow. Rossiter handed her a folded handkerchief which she pressed gratefully to the wound.

Jules groaned again. He looked hideously uncomfortable, with his head twisted on the desk and the terminal keyboard pressing into his stomach. But she was afraid to move him before stopping the bleeding.

Rossiter had unslung his walkie-talkie and was muttering into it. He looked worried. "That's funny. Williams ain't answering the page." He glanced around the room. "No telephone in here. I'll just go phone the police. Want me to get him an ambulance?"

Frankie peeked under the pad. The bleeding had stopped. And Jules was coming around. His eyelids fluttered. She bit her lip indecisively. "Wouldn't it be just as quick to take him in my car?"

"Likely would." Rossiter nodded and came to help her. Between them they got Jules to his feet. He was conscious, but just barely, and it seemed a long way down the corridor. But Rossiter motioned her to go a different way. "Fire door over here," he said as they left the tank. "You go bring your car around, miss. I'll take care of him."

Frankie hesitated, but Rossiter seemed dependable, and she would only be gone a second. She ran around the building and gunned her car, roaring up to the fire door like some race-car driver, she thought wryly. Letting the back seat down, she made the rear of the little station wagon into a bed with the help of the old quilt she kept in it for protecting electronic equipment. Rossiter helped Jules crawl into the back of the car, where he lay down gratefully, closing his eyes and turning his head to the side. Frankie looked at him despairingly. "I should have called an ambulance."

"He'll be all right." Rossiter was oblivious to Frankie's distress. "Better get him to the hospital, though. He don't look concussed, but you never can tell. I'll send the police on over there when they're finished here."

The police. Frankie thought about motives for the destruction all the way to the hospital. Once there, however, she was too busy worrying about Jules, who disappeared into a cubicle with a cheerful young doctor and didn't come out for an hour. She wondered if she should be calling his parents, but before she could decide what to do, a patrolman stopped her restless pacing up and down the hall in front of Jules's cubicle. "Miss Warburton? The hospital staff says you're the one who discovered Julian Jones tonight." His voice was friendly and unthreatening, but Frankie was immediately on her guard. She had her own ideas about who was behind the events of the night, but she didn't know if it was up to her to spill her guts to the police.

The patrolman evidently wasn't interested in her theories. He asked about the HELP message, seeming very interested in the mechanics of sending it. "I understand all the computer equipment in the room was smashed. How would Mr. Jones be able to send this message under those circumstances?"

Frankie let an impatient breath hiss between her teeth, but answered civilly enough. "The microcomputer in the room was smashed, and one of the terminals. The other terminal was hooked into the mainframe computer, the big one that has a room to itself elsewhere. I was also using the mainframe through my telephone at home. All these big computers have provisions for sending and receiving messages among the users. Jules wouldn't have known if there was anyone to get the message, but sending it would be easy, even for someone who'd just been hit on the head. He would type a message code, the message itself and the repeat code. I got it until he evidently fell forward on the keyboard and erased everything."

The patrolman nodded, clearly impressed by her fluency but looking a little confused. He asked her to describe everything she did after receiving the message, and she conscientiously recited her actions, leaving nothing out. Then he snapped his notebook shut and took his leave without asking for her opinion as to who was behind it. For that she was grateful. "Mr. Jeremiah Jones is at the office now, but I understand he's very worried about his son and will be here soon. Thanks for your help, Miss Warburton."

Frankie frowned and chewed a fingernail, watching the patrolman stroll into the cubicle to talk to Jules. She wasn't sure Jules would be in any shape for a scene with his father.

But when Jeremiah Jones bustled down the hallway fifteen minutes later, his evident concern laid her fears to rest. He waited with her in the hall, thanking her gruffly for "saving that fool boy's life," pacing anxiously until the young doctor came out and told them they could see Jules if they wanted to.

They wanted to. Jeremiah tiptoed in, Frankie sheltering behind his bulk. She was suddenly a little shy, uncertain how Jules would take her part in the excitement.

She needn't have worried. Jules was sitting up in the narrow bed, his eyes fastened eagerly on the door. He seemed both touched and surprised by his father's concern and relief at his well-being, but it was Frankie's eyes he sought, her hands he held as if he'd never let them go.

"Don't put me through another night like this one, son." His first effusions over, Jeremiah Jones was quickly reverting to his usual prickly manner. "I'm too old for the scare. Trix wanted to be here but I was afraid she'd be overcome." He pulled Frankie to him for a brief hug and scowled at Jules. "There aren't many young ladies plucky enough to do what Miss Frankie did. Maybe if you two would settle down together you'd have something better to do in the evenings than spending your time with a computer."

Jules squeezed Frankie's hands. "Right, dad. I'll get on it straight away."

Jeremiah looked pleased. Then his face clouded and he cleared his throat. "They've found young Williams, the guard."

Jules didn't take his eyes off Frankie. "Have they?" His voice was indifferent.

Jeremiah raised his eyebrows. "By gad, you take it pretty lightly, son. You evidently got a few licks of your own in on him." He couldn't keep the masculine satisfaction out of his voice. Frankie hid a smile. "He made it to his car, but he was in no shape to drive. The highway patrol pulled him over and he started talking and didn't stop." He cleared his throat again. "Someone hired him—he says he doesn't know who. It was all done over the telephone. Whoever it was, they offered him more money than he could resist."

"Maybe we should pay the guards more," Jules said heedlessly, pulling Frankie down to sit beside him on the narrow bed.

"We aren't going to pay them $5,000 more!" Jeremiah's voice was getting louder, and Frankie shushed him imperatively. "Although—actually that isn't such a bad idea, son." He thought for a moment, and resumed his story. "According to Williams, all he was supposed to do was go in and bash up the equipment a little, and steal your board and drawings. He had no idea you were working late tonight—you must have let yourself in by the front door."

Jules tore his gaze from Frankie's face and nodded. "I went to get a cup of coffee out of the machine, and when I came back he was tearing up the place. I guess he didn't realize I was still working on my terminal—the screen is the kind that blanks out if you leave it for a minute or two. The last thing I remember is thinking of Frankie. It was like that song—I kept thinking, 'I've got to get a message to her.'" A puzzled frown creased his forehead. He raised one hand to touch the bandage on the back of his skull. "I don't remember actually sending the message. The police officer that was just here said I did—said you got it on your home terminal."

Frankie smoothed the hair back from his forehead. They had taken away his horn-rims, and his eyes looked naked and vulnerable. "I was getting ready to send you a message. I knew you were the only one left on the computer, so when the "HELP" came through I figured it must be you." She smiled at him tenderly. "Scared me to death."

Jeremiah nodded in agreement. "Us too, when the police called." He cleared his throat again. "Jules, I don't know if you have any idea about who's behind it all. It was worth a lot of money to someone to sabotage your work."

Jules was silent for a moment. "Who do you think did it, dad?"

Jeremiah moved uneasily. "No idea, my boy. I've got no idea." He spoke bravely, but they all knew it was a lie.

Jules flapped one hand. Suddenly he looked utterly weary. "Do whatever you see fit," he mumbled, his eyes closing. "I don't really care about it."

Frankie and Jeremiah exchanged worried glances. "We'd better go," Frankie said.

Jules's grasp on her hand tightened. "Don't leave me here." His eyes flew open. "I hate hospitals, and I don't have a concussion really. The doctor said it was just a scalp wound and I could go home."

"You can't go off to that boat with no one to look after you, boy!" Jeremiah's voice shed its sickroom gentility and resumed its familiar bullying tone. "You come home with me and let your mother cosset you a bit."

Jules visibly repressed a shudder. "No thanks, dad. I'll be fine." He looked at Frankie. "Can you give me a ride?"

She calmed Jeremiah's protest with a shake of her head. "I'll look after him," she said firmly. "He can stay with me."

Jeremiah brightened, and allowed himself to be

persuaded from the room. He drew Frankie down the hall to a bench. "Wanted to talk to you privately for a minute."

Frankie sat down with him and waited.

"It was Grif, wasn't it?" Jeremiah's voice sounded dull with fatigue when he finally spoke.

Frankie coughed. "It eems to me that there's very little evidence. They may never find out who was behind it all."

"It was Grif though." The older man was positive. "I don't know what gets into those boys," he muttered, his hands moving restlessly over his tweed jacket. "They've been at it tooth and nail for the past ten years."

Frankie put her hand on his arm, wanting to give comfort, but not knowing what to say. "They feel that they're competing," she offered finally. "They both want the same thing."

Jeremiah looked at her, his eyes shrewd beneath jutting brows. "Both want to be top dog, eh? It would serve them right if I went outside for my successor." He sank into thought again, and Frankie waited. At last he stirred and spoke. "I'll take care of Grif," he said, his voice tired. "Guess I should have told them both what I was planning and put their minds at rest. In a way, this is my fault for wanting to play them off against each other."

Frankie tried to object, but he gestured for silence. "I want you to tell the boy this, when you think he's well enough. I have been grooming Grif for the presidency of Jones Morton." She gasped, but he gave her no time to interrupt. "Grif is simply a better businessman than Jules. But—" he held up his hand peremptorily and she forced back her protest "—Jules, as I recall you telling me one day, has something just as important as business sense.

He is creative, innovative and he does come up with the goods. I had thought to spin off an entreprenurial branch of the company with Jules at its head, a kind of super think tank research branch.''

"Why didn't you tell Jules?" Frankie could keep still no longer. "You know," she said sternly, "he feels you favor Grif over him, that you wish Grif was your son."

"Boy's a fool." Jeremiah ran his hands through his thinning hair in agitation. "I couldn't be more proud of him if he was—if he was—" Words failed him.

"Then tell him so." Frankie pulled him to his feet and steered him briskly down the hall toward Jules's cubicle.

"Now?" Jeremiah hung back, but Frankie was adamant.

"Now. He needs to hear it, and you need to say it. But don't stay too long. He needs to rest too."

She pushed Jeremiah into the room and smiled broadly at the young doctor, who was approaching with a clipboard full of papers to sign.

The doctor smiled back. "Your patient will be fine. Got a head as hard as concrete. Make sure he gets plenty of bed rest and doesn't overexert himself. Let him lie around for the next few days. Doubt if he'll feel up to doing much, and that's fine. Bring him in next week, or take him to his own doctor, and have the stitches looked at. He'll be as good as new in no time."

An idea struck Frankie, so revolutionary she was breathless for a moment. The doctor handed her the dismissal paperwork and started to leave. She grabbed his arm.

"Listen—could he go in a car? Now, I mean? For quite a long drive?"

The doctor shrugged. "He's probably going to sleep for the next several hours no matter where he is. A car would be all right if he could lie down and be comfortable. What did you have in mind?"

She didn't answer. "And about not exerting himself. Does that include—I mean, can he—" She felt a blush creeping up her face and fumed at her own dumb maidenly modesty. "Can he have sex?" Her question came out much louder than she had intended. A couple of nurses across the hall looked around and grinned. The doctor grinned too.

"If he's willing, he'll be able. But don't rush him, now. And don't wear him out." He clapped a hand on her shoulder and winked before stepping jauntily away.

Frankie said goodbye to an elated Jeremiah, who came out of his son's cubicle looking as if he'd just been made father of the year. Then she arranged with the nurses to have Jules at the hospital door when she brought her car around. She reclined the front passenger seat and draped the quilt to make a cozy nest.

One of the nurses was just wheeling him up to the doors when she pulled up in front. It would have to be the cute nurse, Frankie thought sourly. She was fussing over him, trying to get him to stay in the wheelchair. He pushed her away as Frankie jumped out of the car.

"I'll walk," he said grimly. When he saw the seat made into a bed, he protested, but Frankie was firm. He was asleep before she'd passed two stoplights.

That suited her plans just fine. She went to his houseboat and packed some clothes for him, rummaging around in his tidy cupboards with a faint feeling of trespass. She left the cabin door open while she packed, running to it often to make sure her car was still where she'd left it, and Jules was still in it. Using the keys that the hospital had collected from his pocket, she locked everything up tightly.

In her workroom at home, her computer was still running. With a slight sense of shock, she realized that it was scarcely two hours since she'd rushed out in fear of Jules's life. She felt as if she'd lived an eternity since then. After turning off her equipment she hauled a suitcase out from under her bed and started piling clothes in it. Sarabeth woke up and came to see what was happening.

"You mean he's out there in the car right now?" Frankie had filled her in as coherently as she could. Excitement was percolating through her veins at the step she was about to take. She'd never done anything so reckless, so risky. But underlying the excitement was a cool confidence that she was making the right move.

"Would you go out and check on him for me? The doctor said he'd just sleep for hours, but I don't want him to be uncomfortable."

Yawning, Sarabeth went out. Frankie finished her packing and lugged the suitcase out to the car. Her roommate was standing by the passenger door, watching Jules with a maternal expression. She raised her brows as Frankie heaved her own suitcase into the back of the car beside Jules's. "I hope you packed a sweater. It gets cold up at Tahoe, even in the summer."

"My, my." Frankie shut the back of the car and smiled at Sarabeth in admiration. "Aren't you the clever little detective."

"Are you okay to drive?" Sarabeth gave Jules one last look. "Let me make you a thermos of coffee. And then, I guess I'll have to get *my* things packed. You won't be wanting a superfluous roommate when you get back from where you're going.''

Frankie had brought out a pillow and another quilt. She adjusted them around Jules and smiled at the cozy picture he made. His pulse was regular, his forehead warm and dry. She hugged Sarabeth affectionately and went around to the driver's side. "We won't evict you. In fact, if we don't live on the *Nautilus*, maybe you'd like to. And I'll stop at a Denny's or something if I need coffee.'' She looked at Jules again. "For the first couple of hours at least, I expect love will keep me awake.''

12

JULES WOKE BRIEFLY as the sun came up over the Sierra Nevadas, when they were on Highway 50 before it descends into the Tahoe Valley. He opened sleepy eyes, glimpsed the towering pines that enclosed the road, breathed deeply of the tangy mountain air and went back to sleep, snuggling into his pillow like a child.

Frankie was beginning to tire. There had been little traffic during the five-hour drive, but the road was winding and precipitous in places, and she had had no sleep. And she knew the hardest task was before her—finding a place to stay at Lake Tahoe on a Saturday morning in the busy summer season. Her sense of confidence faltered. She was just as glad that Jules didn't stay awake. Before she could face the questions he was sure to ask, she needed some rest.

The road curved around the southern end of the huge lake, and she followed it automatically, refreshed in spite of her weariness by the sparkling air and by glimpses of the vast glittering surface of the lake, an impossible-looking deep blue green that spoke of its ancient purity. The road flattened out and the hotels and motels immediately surrounded her with their clamorous signs and promises of entertainment. She drove across the state line and past the endless casinos with a growing sense of panic. Where was the romantic mountain cabin of her imagination? Where was the kindly old justice of the peace? She passed a small building, wildly overornamented with gingerbread trim, exuding the air of a monstrous Victorian gas station. Wedding Chapel, proclaimed a giant sign above it in large fancy lettering. In smaller letters it read, Drive-Thru.

"Oh dear, oh dear," Frankie muttered under her breath, driving numbly on.

"What's the matter?"

Jules's voice made her jump. He sat up beside her, shedding blankets, and groped for the knob that would crank the seat up.

"I—I thought you would sleep longer. How do you feel?" His color was good, she saw, stealing a glance at him. He yawned and winced, feeling the bandage ruefully.

"I feel great, except for a headache." He looked out the window and then at her, his face expressionless. "We're in Tahoe, aren't we?"

"Well," Frankie said nervously, "you're right. That's just where we are." He waited, and she added finally, "I thought we could use a little vacation. Really get away from it all for a while."

"Have you been driving all night?" His voice was quiet, and she thought she could detect a faint hint of amusement. Relieved, she began to babble.

"Yes, I have. It wasn't too bad, actually. I mean, I often do stay up all night to work on a problem, so it was nothing, you know."

He looked at his wrist. "Where's my watch? It must be early."

She fished around one-handed on the floor under his feet. "The hospital put all your valuables in this envelope here. And it is early. It's not even eight yet. I guess that's why the traffic is so light—"

He interrupted her a little sternly. "It sounds like you need a break for a while. Why don't we stop for breakfast?"

"Good idea." Gregariously she swept her hand across the car. "You pick a place and I'll stop."

He scanned the signs. "There!" he said suddenly. "Pull in here."

She skidded to a halt and pulled in where he'd indicated, narrowly missing a car parked to the left. "But—this isn't a restaurant."

"No, it's not." They both stared out the front windshield at the small weathered building. A sign in front of it proclaimed it the office of the justice of the peace for the county.

"It—it's not open yet," Frankie said stupidly. Jules took her chin in his hand and turned her to face him. Her knees began to tremble. The look in his eyes was like nourishment for her heart.

"I've waited a long time. I can wait for another thirty-five minutes." He cupped her face in his hands and brought his lips to hers. Lightning shot through her, and earthquakes and thunder. When their lips parted at last she was surprised, in a dazed sort of way, that the day was still placid. "Oh, Frankie," he sighed against her lips. "I've missed you so much. I love you so much. Let's not fight anymore. Let's get married and have a family, and spend all our time together."

Frankie closed her eyes blissfully, but opened them a second later in dismay. "Oh, Jules! I wanted to be the one to propose. Oh, rats!"

"Never mind," he said soothingly, "you picked the time and place." He looked thoughtfully out the window. "I hate to be practical or anything, but did you also think to reserve some tiny spot where we can consummate our approaching nuptials?"

For some reason his words struck her as supremely funny. "Consummate our—what a card you are, Jones!" She sobered and turned to look at him. "I didn't," she admitted. "That's what I was bemoaning when you woke up. Somehow none of these motels fit my ideal of a honeymoon cottage."

He searched the manila envelope for his keys. "Not to worry," he said briskly. "Dad has a little place up here complete with private beach and boat, and I believe I still have my key to it—yes, this looks like it." He consulted his watch again. "So that makes thirty minutes for breakfast, another half hour to get married and then—eternity!"

"Listen." Frankie had another thought. "That doctor—he said you weren't supposed to overexert yourself."

"I heard what he said." Jules grinned at her devilishly. "I also heard your not-so-subtle question," he added. "It certainly helped to set my mind at rest about your feelings toward me."

"You're a cad to let on you heard me," Frankie murmured, running her hands through the crisp curls of his hair. "Why do I love you, I wonder." She tweaked his nose and added saucily, "Let me count the ways."

"The reasons." He sighed contentedly. "You mean, let you count the reasons. We'll turn you into a poetry lover yet."

"I just want to be a poet's lover," Frankie whispered. She trailed her fingers down his throat, pausing on the pulse point. It leaped under her touch like a trout in a stream. "Don't get too worked up, or we'll have to postpone the honeymoon."

THE JUSTICE OF THE PEACE was a courtly, white-haired old gentleman with beautiful handwriting. They had no rings, and Frankie's bouquet had been hastily gleaned by Jules from the planter box in front of the restaurant. But the judge pronounced them man and wife despite their lack of the proper nuptial accessories, filling out the marriage certificate in first-rate style. And the cabin owned by Jules's father was small but charmingly rustic, its unfinished walls punctuated by wide, many-paned windows that gave a beautiful view of Lake Tahoe.

"No hot tub?" Frankie bounced on the bed in the downstairs bedroom and glanced through to the small bathroom with its practical fixtures.

Jules had insisted on carrying his own suitcase in. At that moment he sat heavily beside her, and she saw with alarm that he looked pale. She jumped up and began unpacking the bags, thinking furiously. After putting the last garment in the drawer, she stretched and yawned.

"Jules, darling, I'm sorry—" She yawned again, making a very artistic effort of it. "I'm simply dropping from all that driving I did...." Turning, she saw that her act had been unnecessary. Jules was sprawled on the bed, his chest rising and falling in even rhythm, his horn-rims askew on his nose.

She took off the glasses and put them on the bedside table. His pants came off pretty easily once she'd taken his shoes off. Since his arms were crossed on his chest, she left his T-shirt on. Removing her own clothes, she curled beside him on the bed and drew the covers over them. "My husband," she murmured drowsily. He stirred and turned so they were lying like spoons, her back curved into his front. She clasped his arm under her breasts and slept.

There was a butterfly brushing her cheek with

sweet light touches, and she smiled in pleasure. Then the butterfly's touch fluttered over her lips, drawing a response that began to quicken in her like fire. She moaned, and the feathery caress slipped inside her mouth, sipping her nectar. Her eyes still closed, she raised her hand and encountered the slightly scratchy stubble of Jules's chin.

"Mmmm," she sighed, opening her eyes. He had taken off the rest of his clothes and hung over her, smiling at her with heart-stopping intensity.

"How will you ever forgive me for sacking out at the start of our honeymoon?" His voice was rueful.

"Let me count the ways," she whispered, pulling his mouth down to hers again. Their tongues met and danced together, punctuated by her soft moans and his whispered love words. She stroked the smoothly muscled skin of his back, her palms reveling in the sensations. His own hands wandered sweetly down her body, pausing at all the right places, as if on a voyage of rediscovery. He sent his mouth after them, drawing first one nipple, then the other, into his mouth for slow, voluptuous sucking. Frankie's body began to move, arching against him with ever-increasing demand.

But Jules was in no hurry. "Slow down, love," he panted in her ear. "Remember, I have to take things... very easy." He drew back for a moment to look at her, his eyes bright with passion. "God, you look wonderful!" He filled his hands with her hair, bringing it around to fall gently over her breasts. The swollen nipples pushed through the golden rain, pleading for more caresses. He closed his eyes in momentary wonder. "You are—so beautiful."

"So are you," Frankie murmured, gazing at him with love-filled eyes. The strong sleek planes of his chest invited her touch. She stroked the throbbing pulse that beat in his neck, tangled her fingers in the crisp hair that curled around his flat male nipples. She teased each nipple gently with her fingernails, taking pleasure in Jules's indrawn breath and suddenly taut body. More boldly she followed the tapering line of his stomach.

He groaned and rolled onto his back, pulling her on top of him. "I'm a sick man," he said huskily. "You do all the work." As if to belie his words, his hands cupped the weight of her breasts, his thumb and forefinger tugging gently on the nipples until they rose tensely, begging for the solace of his mouth. Frankie swayed forward, brushing his face with her breasts until he captured one swollen nipple between his lips, soothing it with his tongue, then sending flashes of excitement through her by nibbling gently all around it. She moaned in protest when he stopped, but he paused only long enough to gaze with fierce satisfaction at her melting eyes before giving her other breast the treatment it demanded.

She sent her hands with increasing urgency over his body, drawing fiery patterns on his skin with fingers that felt as incendiary as if they were glowing. She slid her smooth body down his rough hairy one, moving teasingly against his insistent hardness. He gasped and she sat up, feeling suddenly powerful, glorying in the way she could make him respond. His hands trailed down her body, his fingers unerringly finding the damp inner heat that craved completion. With a savage moan he arched upward. Their bodies met in primeval force that sent passionate reverberations throughout them. They fell together, letting the storm sweep them far, far away, until they were lapped finally in the gentler waves of fulfillment.

His hand stroked idly through her hair, smoothing the silken tresses away from her face. Holding each other close, they kissed tenderly. When the kiss began to escalate, Frankie pulled away.

"No more for you," she said firmly. "Remember what the doctor said."

"I can't remember," Jules growled, reaching for her. "I forgot already."

"That's because you have a head injury." Frankie jumped up and searched for her clothes. "I only married you because I'm in love with your brain. So don't run any risks with it, buddy. The day you can't remember Maxwell's equations is the day I walk."

Jules scratched his head in bewilderment. "Let's see now, that's πR^2, isn't it? I remember that one," he confided, "because I always thought pie are round, you know? Isn't it wonderful what science can do?"

"Dolt!" Frankie leaped for the bed and subdued him after a brief scuffle. "Repeat after me," she ordered fiercely. "$E - mc^2$."

"$E - mc^2$," he said obediently.

"Good. Now repeat this: $F + J -$ infinity."

He smiled at her. "I'll carve it on every tree I see. Frankie, you know I'm as old-fashioned about divorce as I am about abortion. I don't want it anywhere near me."

Frankie sighed with deep happiness. "Great, Jones, because neither do I." She kissed him with a loud smack of her lips and bounded off the bed, feeling full of energy and vitality. "Say, do you suppose your dad might have left a Twinkie or a Ding-dong around here somewhere? I'm famished!"

THE AUTHOR

Leigh Roberts is a transplanted midwesterner who currently lives in California with her engineer husband and two small sons. She overcame her distrust of technology by researching and writing *Love Circuits* and is now at work on another Harlequin Temptation.

Books by Leigh Roberts

HARLEQUIN TEMPTATION
20–LOVE CIRCUITS

HARLEQUIN SUPERROMANCE
81–MOONLIGHT SPLENDOR

These books may be available at your local bookseller.

For a list of all titles currently available,
send your name and address to:

Harlequin Reader Service
P.O. Box 52040, Phoenix, AZ 85072-2040
Canadian address: P.O. Box 2800, Postal Station A,
5170 Yonge St., Willowdale, Ont. M2N 5T5

INTRODUCING

Harlequin Temptation

Sensuous...contemporary...compelling...reflecting today's lov
relationships! The passionate
torment of a woman torn betwe
two loves...the siren call of a ca
...the magnetic advances of an
impetuous employer–nothing i
left unexplored in this romant
new series from Harlequin. Y
thrill to a candid new frankn
as men and women seek to l
lasting relationships in the
of temptations that threat
true love. *Don't miss a single*
You can start new *Harleq
Temptation* coming to your
home each month for j
$1.75 per book–a savin
20¢ off the suggested
price of $1.95. Begin
your FREE copy of F
Impressions. Mail the
card today!

First Impressions
by Maris Soule

He was involved with her best friend! Tracy Dexter couldn't
deny her attraction to her new boss. Mark Prescott looked
more like a jet set playboy than a high school principal–and h
acted like one, too. It wasn't right for Tracy to go out with hi
not when her friend Rose had already staked a claim. It wasn
right, even though Mark's eyes were so persuasive, his kiss s
probing and intense. Even though his hands scorched her bo
with a teasing, raging fire...and when he gently lowered her
the floor she couldn't find the words to say no.

A word of warning to our regular readers: While Harlequin books are always
good taste, you'll find more sensuous writing in new *Harlequin Temptation* than
other Harlequin romance series.

® ™Trademarks of Harlequin Enterprises Ltd.

Harlequin Photo ~ *Calendar* ~

Turn Your Favorite Photo into a Calendar.

JULY 1984

The Browns

Uniquely yours, this 10x17½ calendar features your favorite photograph, with any name you wish in attractive lettering at the bottom. A delightfully personal and practical idea.

Send us your favorite color print, black-and-white print, negative, or slide, any size (we'll return it), along with 3 proofs of purchase (coupon below) from a June or July release of Harlequin Romance, Harlequin Presents, Harlequin Superromance, Harlequin American Romance or Harlequin Temptation, plus $5. (includes shipping and handling).

Harlequin Photo Calendar Offer
(PROOF OF PURCHASE)

NAME_____
(Please Print)

ADDRESS_____

CITY_____ STATE_____ ZIP_____

NAME ON CALENDAR_____

Mail photo, 3 proofs, plus check or money order for $5.75 payable to:

Harlequin Books
P.O. Box 52020
Phoenix, AZ 85072

Offer expires December 31, 1984. (Not available in Canada)